Peanut Jones

and the
Illustrated
City.

Jones

Written and illustrated by

ROB BIDDULPH

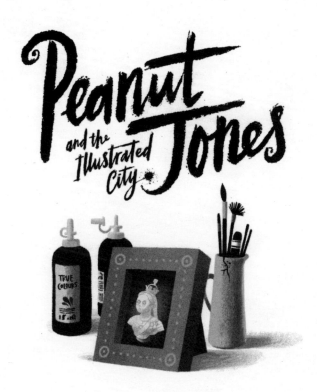

MACMILLAN CHILDREN'S BOOKS

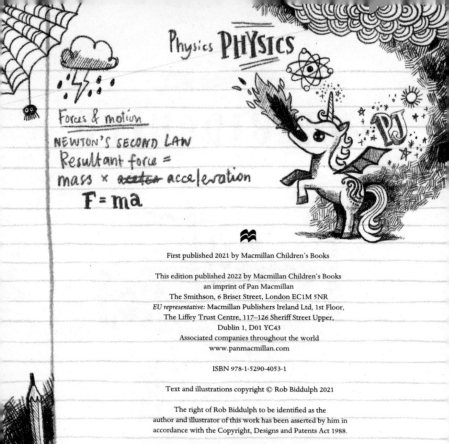

Physics PHYSICS

Forces & motion

NEWTON'S SECOND LAW
Resultant force =
mass × ~~accel~~ acceleration

$$F = ma$$

First published 2021 by Macmillan Children's Books

This edition published 2022 by Macmillan Children's Books
an imprint of Pan Macmillan
The Smithson, 6 Briset Street, London EC1M 5NR
EU representative: Macmillan Publishers Ireland Ltd, 1st Floor,
The Liffey Trust Centre, 117–126 Sheriff Street Upper,
Dublin 1, D01 YC43
Associated companies throughout the world
www.panmacmillan.com

ISBN 978-1-5290-4053-1

3 5 7 9 8 6 4 2

A CIP catalogue record for this book is available from the British Library.

Printed and bound by CPI Group (UK) Ltd, Croydon CR0 4YY

HI!

MIX
Paper | Supporting
responsible forestry
FSC® C116313
FSC
www.fsc.org

For Jodie,
who made it all happen

arithmetic tells me that you have only completed four hundred and ninety-six of the five hundred you were charged with writing. That is 99.2 per cent of your target. As you know, any pupil lucky enough to attend St Hubert's School for the Seriously Scientific and Terminally Mathematic is expected to fulfil every aspect of all tasks that they undertake. One. Hundred. Per cent. In this instance, it is clear that you are 0.8 per cent short of hitting that target.'

A smug smile was developing somewhere behind his crisp-littered beard.

'As punishment for trying to get away with doing less work, not only will you complete the task in full, but you will also write an extra hundred lines. That should give me enough time to finish my crossword, eat this Scotch egg and get home in time for *University Challenge*.'

'But, sir—'

'No buts, Jones. Get it done. I don't know what kind of namby-pamby slacking they tolerated at your previous school, but you need to realise that precision is important. Frivolous creativity has no place at St Hubert's. No place at all.'

2
Rockwell Riley

As Peanut trudged through the school gates, she spotted a tall, rangy boy with a perfect sphere of black hair exploding from the top of his head waiting for her at the bus stop. As soon as he saw her, Rockwell Riley smiled, stood up and tossed her an apple.

'Thought you might want a snack.'

'Thanks,' she sighed, 'but you really didn't need to hang around.'

'Oh, that's OK. I did some chemistry revision while I was waiting. Atomic structure is *so* interesting, don't you think? Did you know that when sodium reacts with non-metals, like chlorine, it totally loses its outer electron? The entire shell surrounding it just disappears, leaving absolutely nothing. Not a sausage. Nada. I mean, talk about mind blown!'

Peanut looked at him blankly 'I have literally no idea what you're talking about,' she said.

'Yeah, right,' said Rockwell, smiling. 'You don't fool me. You like to hide it, but I reckon you're smarter than the rest of us put together. Is that why you're not keen on this whole Study Buddy thing – in case you accidentally let slip how super-clever you are?'

Peanut sighed. St Hubert's Study Buddy scheme was designed to help new students settle in at the school. Buddies were supposed to meet up for an hour each day to discuss any issues that the new pupil might have, but ever since she and Rockwell had been paired up on her first day two months earlier, he had become her shadow. Still, Peanut always tried to dodge the session. She suspected that Rockwell had been assigned to her as much for his benefit as hers because, as far as she could tell, he didn't have any friends at the school. She wasn't sure why, as he seemed perfectly nice. Had she been in the market for a new friend, she could certainly have done a lot worse.

But she wasn't, and that's all there was to it. Peanut had no intention of settling in at St Hubert's, study buddy or no study buddy, because, as far as she was concerned, she wasn't going to be staying for long.

'Listen, you missed our session again today. If lunchtime is a problem, how about we meet up in the morning before school?' said Rockwell, eyes wide with hope. 'What about tomorrow? We don't want to get into trouble for missing it again, do we?'

Another sigh. Knowing he wouldn't give up until she agreed to meet him, Peanut surrendered.

'OK then. If we must.'

'Really? Amazing!' Rockwell's face flushed with pleasure. 'I'll, er, I'll call for you at around eight then, shall I? Melody Road, isn't it?'

'Yes.' She exhaled, loudly. 'Number eighty.'

3
Nerys and the Big Car

s Peanut bit into the apple, an enormous silver car with blacked-out windows turned into the road and sped towards them.

Peanut and Rockwell instinctively stood to attention as it glided to a halt. The rear window slid open to reveal a face Peanut knew well.

'Hiya, lovely.'

Peanut grinned. It was Nerys, her mother's PA at the accountancy firm. Peanut liked her. She was the only one at Mum's work who spoke to her like a normal person rather than a baby.

Peanut had no idea how old Nerys was. Her hair was the sort of lilac colour that immediately places a person in the seventy-something bracket, but her face was remarkably unlined, except for a few small creases at the corners of each eye. Smile lines. Nerys smiled a lot.

'Your mam sent me to fetch you. She got a teletext message from the school saying you were in detention, so here I am. I don't know, those teachers are always grizzling about something, aren't they?'

Nerys opened the car door.

'Now then, lovely, I'm gagging for a cup of tea. So, hurry up, get yourself in here and we'll be back at the office quicker than you can say Llanfairpwllgwyngyllgogerychwyrndrob-wllllantysiliogogogoch.'

Nerys's pale eyes flicked over towards Rockwell.

'Would your little friend like a lift somewhere?'

'Oh-oh,' spluttered Rockwell. 'Th-th-thank you, but no

thank you, madam. Er, m'am. Er, Y-your Highness. I've got my skateboard. I'll see you in the morning, Peanut.' And with that he kicked off and disappeared down the street.

'Aw, he seems nice,' said Nerys, as Peanut climbed in. 'I'm glad you're finally making friends at St Hubert's.'

'Rockwell's not my friend. He's only being nice to me cos he's been told to by the school and he doesn't want to get in trouble. Anyway, I don't *want* to make friends at St Hubert's.' Peanut's eyes filled with tears. '"Friends" implies that I'm having a nice time and don't mind staying. And I am definitely *not* staying.' She looked out of the window. 'It doesn't matter

anyway. Dad will come back home soon. He'll sort everything out with Mum, and then I can go back to my old friends at Melody High.'

Nerys frowned. 'My dearest girl, don't forget that your mam only sent you to St Hubert's because she wants what's best for you. She loves you, y'know. Don't give up on this school just yet, lovely. Things can always change.' She turned to the man in the front seat. 'Drive on, Hammond . . .'

4
Packed Lunch Post-it Notes

It was hard for Peanut to put into words how much she missed her dad. He had disappeared a year ago, and not a minute went by without her wishing with all her might that he'd walk into the room, scoop her up in his arms and give her one of his famous bear hugs. Every single time she heard a phone ring or saw a door open, she half expected it to be him. Each time that it wasn't, she felt the pain of his absence anew. Peanut's dad was an artist, like her. A painter, to be more precise. And he was good – or at least Peanut thought he was. She had inherited her passion for drawing and creating art from him. He was her hero.

She'd loved hanging out in the small,

bright conservatory at the back of the house that Dad had used as a studio. It had been chaotic, but always full of the most interesting objects: half-empty tubes of paint, old mugs filled with paintbrushes, colour charts Sellotaped to walls, poseable wooden dolls, and easels of every size imaginable. But best of all were the paintings, which had been scattered all over the studio.

Some were finished, some were half-finished and some looked finished, only to have been crossed out at the last minute. Peanut loved them all, but her absolute favourites were the empty canvases. Paintings yet to be. There was something so magical about them. Every time she saw that expanse of pure white, she knew that her dad would soon turn it into something more. Something new. She'd felt so lucky to have a father who could conjure beauty out of thin air.

And then there were the Post-it notes.

When she was little, Peanut had been very nervous about leaving nursery and starting school. At nursery, she'd only had to stay for the morning, whereas at school she would have to stay for the whole day. She'd been dreading it. She would miss the fun afternoons she and Dad had spent together and she'd cried for a week in the build-up. Her parents had been very worried.

'I've got an idea,' Mum had said, the day before Peanut was due to start. 'What if, every day, Daddy draws you a little picture on a Post-it note and we put it in your lunchbox? That way, you'll have something to look forward to all morning, and something to laugh about all afternoon. I think it will really help.'

And just like that, Peanut's Packed Lunch Post-it Note Collection started. Every day, her dad would draw her a picture on a small square of yellow paper and hide it among the sandwiches, yogurts and fruit bars. She couldn't wait to see what she would get each day. He drew pictures of her favourite

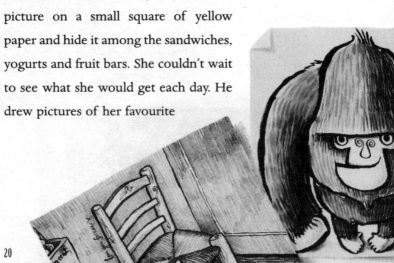

characters from books, TV shows and films, portraits of family members, mini versions of famous paintings and much more besides. Anything and everything Dad could think of. And every single one would have the words 'Love you forever x' hidden somewhere within the drawing.

Throughout the whole of primary school and the start of her time at Melody High, Dad didn't miss a single day, and Peanut treasured every note. She would carefully bring them home each afternoon and put them in a plastic bag under her bed. Then, last year, Dad made a special wooden box for her to store them in and 'keep them all safe'.

'Why "Little Tail"?' she had asked, reading the inscription on the box.

'Well,' he'd replied, '*pencillus*, the Latin word for "artist's paintbrush", translates to "Little Tail" in English. It's also where the word "pencil" originally comes from. I thought it was appropriate considering a paintbrush and a pencil is mainly what I use when I draw them for you.'

Peanut still had the box, full to the brim with more than 2,000 drawings. Of course, there had been no new Post-it notes since Dad had gone. In fact, the daily reminder of his absence she got when she opened her lunchbox to find no drawing inside was like a knife to her heart. Lunchtime had gone from being the best time of day to the worst. Every day, she asked herself the same question: *Where is he?*

5

The Disappearance

It had been baffling when Dad had left.

Peanut, her mum, her brother and her sister had all been to visit Auntie Jean. Dad had decided to stay at home and finish a particularly tricky painting of a sausage dog playing the violin.

'You lot leave me to it,' he'd said, 'To be honest, I don't particularly feel the need to be told what Jean's friend Jackie's brother's boss's aunt's plumber's sister's dog has been up to in the local park. I'm happy for you to fill me in on the details when you get home.'

When they'd got home, however, all they'd found was a note on the dining table.

Straight away, Peanut's older brother Leo had tried to

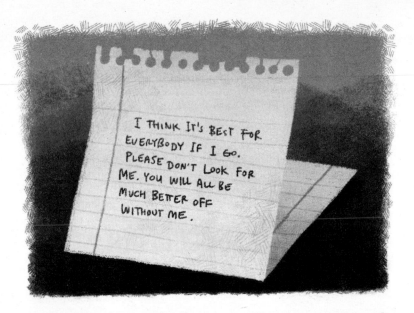

I THINK IT's BEST FOR
EVERYBODY IF I GO.
PLEASE DON'T LOOK FOR
ME. YOU WILL ALL BE
MUCH BETTER OFF
WITHOUT ME.

call him, but when he'd rung Dad's phone, Mum had found it buzzing away in the hallway. She'd then got in touch with everybody she could think of: his friends; Granny; Uncle Ed; but no one had seen or heard anything of Dad. Everyone agreed that it was very out of character, and not one person had seen anything to indicate that this was something he'd been planning. It was all very strange.

Peanut had known straight away that it didn't add up. Firstly, Dad had seemed perfectly happy when they'd left that morning. He'd even joked about how boring it would be at Auntie Jean's! Secondly, why would he leave forever and not take anything (except his passport – that was missing) with him? Surely, he would've at least grabbed his phone, his wallet and a change of clothes? It didn't make any sense.

But more than anything, she just didn't believe he would leave them like that. Not without explaining why. Not without saying goodbye. He was *such* a great dad – always interested in what his kids were up to, always happy to talk through any problems, always putting on silly voices and telling terrible dad jokes. Also, as far as she could tell, he and Mum were really happy. They held hands at every opportunity, and hardly ever argued about whose turn it was to put the bins out, unlike Mr and Mrs Herbert from next door.

Initially, Mum must have felt the same way, because that evening she'd called the police. Peanut heard her tell them over the phone that, yes, he had been acting slightly strangely for the last couple of months. He'd seemed a bit preoccupied with something and had taken to nipping out for an hour or two without telling her where he was going. She'd told them that she'd assumed it was because Dad hadn't sold a painting for a long time and he'd felt a bit down about it.

After a day or so of investigating, a police check with passport control revealed that he had boarded a flight to Mexico on the day of his disappearance. The police had told Mum that, in their opinion, there was no suspicion of any foul play, and it seemed to be a simple case of someone running away from his responsibilities. Dad would get in contact with them when he was ready, they'd said.

And, apparently, they were right. Two days later, Mum received this postcard from Mexico City:

That was the moment that Mum switched from feeling worried to feeling angry. *Very* angry.

'How could he do this to us? So *selfish!*' She shook her head. 'How could I not have noticed that something was wrong? I know I've been working a lot lately, but still . . .'

Peanut wasn't having it. She'd been certain that there was something fishy going on. For a start, why would he travel all the way to Mexico without any money? Also, it was obvious to her that the handwriting on the note wasn't quite right. Dad never wrote in capital letters. Surely this was enough evidence to arouse at least a *tiny* bit of suspicion? Why weren't the police and, more importantly, Mum doing more to find him?

'In the last forty-eight hours I've learned a lot about your father,' Mum had explained to Peanut and Leo, after she'd put their sister to bed. 'Yesterday, I went through the browser history on his laptop and it's quite obvious that he's been planning this for months. Look.'

She'd shown them several web pages with headlines like *How to start a new life* and *Ten signs that it's time to leave your wife and family*.

'NO!' Peanut had shouted. 'That's just not true. He wouldn't. Not Dad!'

At that point, Leo had left the room without saying a word and disappeared upstairs.

'Face it, Peanut,' said Mum sadly. 'Your father just isn't the person we thought he was. We've all been living a lie for months, maybe even years.'

'Well, I don't believe it.' Peanut was crying by then. 'My dad would never, EVER leave us. He just wouldn't! We need to find him.'

'Oh sweetheart, I don't know what to think any more,' Mum had said, pulling Peanut in for a cuddle. 'I really don't.'

Two months passed with no word from Dad, and each week Mum's anger levels had gone up a notch. Then, one day, she'd decided to put all of Dad's painting paraphernalia in the shed. 'Time to get rid of this rubbish!' she'd said. 'He's obviously not coming back. We might as well make proper use of the conservatory.'

Another few months went by before Mum had dropped the bombshell.

'Peanut, I've decided to take you out of Melody High and send you to St Hubert's.'

'What? Why?!' Peanut had shouted. Her school was the one thing that had kept her going through the trauma of Dad disappearing. 'I love it at Melody and I'm doing really well. My art teacher says I'm starting to show some real promise.'

'Drawing and painting are all well and good, Peanut,' snapped Mum. 'It's a nice thing to do as a hobby, but you can't make a career out of it. Look at your dad. All that creativity ruined him. It sucked the ambition and the drive out of him. In the end, he had absolutely no get up and go. Well, not until he got up and went, at least.'

'But Mum . . .'

'Look, people at work tell me that they've heard good things about St Hubert's maths department,' said Mum, looking determined. 'And the science faculty is second to none in terms of results. That's the area you should be concentrating on.'

'That's so unfair! What about Leo?'

'Leo has his exams this year and I don't want to disrupt him. Besides, I'm less worried about the direction in which he's headed.' Mum had set her jaw.

'I'm sorry, Peanut, I've made up my mind. St Hubert's has agreed to give you a place. I have paid the fees for the first year and you start next week.'

So, that's how Peanut Jones came to be sitting in the back of a chauffeur-driven car, next to her mother's personal assistant, having been collected from a school she hates, after doing a detention for drawing a picture of a fire-breathing vampire unicorn in her physics book.

6
Blood, Stone & Partners

The building that housed her mother's accountancy firm always made Peanut feel tiny. It towered so high it felt like it might fall forwards and crush her at any second.

'Your mam won't be long and then you two can head off home,' said Nerys as she shuffled towards the building and triggered automatic sliding doors. 'We can go up and wait in her office. I'll get that kettle on.'

Peanut's mum had worked at Blood, Stone & Partners for just over three years. Peanut could clearly remember the day that

Mum had got the job, mainly because Dad had nipped to the shop to buy a bottle of champagne and some cream soda for the children. Peanut, Leo and their baby sister were *never* allowed to have fizzy drinks so this had been *very* exciting.

'Here's to my wife, the high-flying accountant!' Dad had shouted, beaming with pride as he and Mum clinked their glasses together. 'I always knew you could do it!'

What a happy day that was. It seemed like a long time ago now.

Peanut and Nerys walked out of the lift and headed down the long glass corridor towards Mum's office. Peanut counted sixteen doors on each side, each one leading to an identical cube-shaped room housing an identical desk, an identical chair and an identical computer screen. They were all empty. She wondered how each member of staff remembered which one was theirs.

At the end of the corridor was a large wooden door with a gold plaque on it.

TRACEY JONES
DIRECTOR OF FORENSIC
ACCOUNTING

Nerys knocked and then walked in without waiting for an answer. Peanut followed.

In contrast to the glass labyrinth outside, Mum's office felt very old-fashioned. For a start, the walls, floor and ceiling were all covered with exactly the same type of wood. It immediately made Peanut feel drowsy, as if she were being given a great big oaky cuddle. It was also slightly disorientating, as it was quite easy to forget which way was up and which way was down. This wasn't helped by the fact that the room had no windows. What little light there was came from either

the massive circular iron chandelier that held ten fake candles and looked like it had been stolen from the set of *Game of Thrones*, or the eighty-inch flat screen embedded into one of the walls. The TV only ever seemed to show one channel: BBN (Big Business News). As far as Peanut could tell, it exclusively featured very grey people, in very grey suits, talking endlessly about the never-ending river of seemingly random numbers that flowed along the bottom of the screen. *What a waste,* thought Peanut. *If I worked here I'd watch Marvel films all day long.*

Mum was sitting in a dark-green leather swivel chair behind her desk, a massive mahogany monstrosity with edges inlaid with a mother-of-pearl Celtic knot design. She was furiously tapping away at a laptop.

Without looking up, she said, 'Hello, darling. I'm nearly finished. Have a seat and Nerys will get you a cup of tea. We'll talk about your detention later.'

Peanut sat down in an armchair next to another much smaller desk in the corner of the room. Nerys approached the wall next to Peanut and pushed one of the panels. To Peanut's delight, it opened up to reveal a small but immaculate kitchen. Nerys went in and filled up the kettle.

The desk Peanut was sitting next to was much messier than Mum's. Pens and pencils were strewn across it and several ledgers were lying open with corners of pages folded over. At the front, there was what looked like a black plastic Toblerone bar with the words 'Nerys Jenkins, PA to DFA' printed on it. Peanut picked up a pencil and started doodling absent-mindedly on one of the pads. Then she noticed Nerys's computer. The screen was covered with yellow Post-it notes, each one completely filled with writing and little tick boxes.

A wave of sadness hit Peanut. The sight of those small yellow squares of paper made her miss Dad terribly.

The sound of Mum's office door slamming woke Peanut from her daydream with a jolt. A very handsome, very short man wearing a black suit, a black shirt, black shoes and a black tie covered with very, very, very dark grey polka dots strode confidently into the room.

When he spoke, his voice was much higher than Peanut had expected it to be. 'Tracey darling, how are you getting on with that report summarising your investigation into the possible VAT carousel fraud involving Globetown Limited? I need to get Blood's eyes on it first thing in the morning.'

Since starting at St Hubert's, Peanut was getting used to hearing sentences that made absolutely no sense whatsoever, but this one was on another level. *What in the name of Mary Poppins is 'carousel fraud'?* she thought. Maybe somebody was attempting to con fairground-goers by passing off a roundabout as a merry-go-round.

'Nearly there, Milton,' said Mum in a strange voice that Peanut didn't recognise. 'I just need to give it a final read-through overnight.'

'Ah. And who might this be?' The man turned to face Peanut, and the perfumed pomade in his slicked-back hair reflected the flickering light from the *Game of Thrones* chandelier. He looked her up and down with his pale grey eyes.

'Oh. This is my daughter, Pea— Er, Pernilla. Pernilla, this is Milton Stone. My boss.'

Peanut knew all about Milton Stone. She knew that he had been at university with Mum twenty years earlier. She knew they had studied maths together. She also suspected that he had plans for a romantic relationship with Mum now that Dad was out of the picture. Why else would he have called her 'darling'? The thought of that happening made her feel physically sick.

'Pernilla? Great name.' His high voice was as oily as his hair. 'And I see you've been doodling on one of our legal pads. Budding artist, eh?'

'Sort of,' grunted Peanut. She was still reeling from him calling her mum *darling* and the whole *Pernilla* thing.

'I'll just run and get the printouts of the report,' said Mum, as she hurried out of the room towards one of the glass cubes down the corridor.

Stone glanced at Nerys, who was busy scribbling something on yet another Post-it note, and then turned back to Peanut. He snatched the legal pad from her, tore off the piece of paper that she had drawn on, screwed it up and threw it in the bin.

'Little girl, please refrain from wasting the pages of my legal pads by populating them with your scribblings,' he snarled. 'Paper doesn't grow on trees, you know! And my team needs these pads for *real* work.'

Mum returned to the room, and Stone's manner changed instantly.

'Charming child, Tracey. Utterly charming. And what vivid red hair. Very striking.'

Mum looked surprised. 'Er, what a nice thing to say. Say thank you to Mr Stone, Pea— Er, Pernilla.'

Peanut was silent, partly because she was reeling from the second *Pernilla*.

'Pernilla! What do you say . . . ?' hissed Mum.

'Thanks,' she muttered.

'Not at all.' Stone grinned. 'Not at all. Tracey, I'll look forward to seeing that report on my desk at nine a.m. tomorrow morning. Thanks awfully, darling.'

And with that he left the office and marched off down the glass corridor.

Peanut stared after him. 'Actually, paper *does* grow on trees,' she whispered.

8
Leo

'We've arrived, madam.'

'Thanks, Hammond. Would you like to pop in for a quick cup of tea?'

'That's very kind of you, madam, but I have to head back to the office to take Mr Stone home.' His deep voice was warm and soothing. 'He'll probably finish work at some point in the next four hours and I have to be ready and waiting or, ahem, y'know . . .' Hammond made the slitting-throat gesture with his hand.

'Yes. Of course. Well, thanks for the lift.'

'I'm at your service, madam. And very nice to meet you, young miss.'

'You too.' Peanut smiled at him.

The Jones family had lived at 80 Melody Road for the past fifteen years. It was an unremarkable medium-sized Victorian terraced house, its only distinguishing feature a bright yellow front door and window frames painted to match. Mum and Peanut walked up the black-and-white tiled path and went inside.

'We're home!' shouted Mum as they entered the hallway. 'Everything OK?'

A low, flat voice from somewhere at the back of the house replied. 'Everything's fine.'

It was Leo, Peanut's older brother.

Leo was sixteen and, like his mother, maths was his thing. Specifically, something called *pure* maths which, Peanut imagined, was like normal maths but somehow even more mathsy. Maths squared. His dream was to become a theoretical mathematician when he was older.

When Peanut had asked him what a theoretical mathematician was, he'd got very excited and said: 'Well, it's somebody who tries to figure out the answers to maths questions that nobody else has been able to figure out the answers to before.'

'Why would anybody ever want to waste time doing that?' Peanut had said. 'I'd just ask a teacher!'

'Ha! Believe it or not, Topknot –' Peanut liked it when he called her that – 'there are some questions that even teachers don't know the answers to. In fact, sometimes, a theoretical mathematician will have to spend more time working out what the question is in the first place, than they will finding the answer.'

'OK, you're scaring me now.'

'Ha. No, it's actually *really* interesting. And it can be applied in loads of different ways to help in real-life situations. Maybe a doctor needs to calculate the rate at which a particular disease is going to spread, or an engineer needs to know how to make a certain type of boat float. I might be able to work it out for them with a brand-new maths equation that I invent.'

'So you're saying that by telling them what seven times six is, you'll be able to make a ship sail to Timbuktu? Whatever you say, *Pythagoras*.'

This banter would often go on for hours, sometimes accompanied by wrestling, always accompanied by laughter.

But Leo didn't laugh very often these days. Not since Dad left. In fact, he had changed beyond all recognition over the course of the last year, and was no longer the wise-cracking, fun-loving brother that Peanut was so fond of. He wore a permanently anxious expression and had separated himself almost entirely from the rest of the family. He spent most of the time either alone in his bedroom, or out with friends.

Peanut couldn't remember the last time he had called her Topknot.

Little-Bit

'EEEEEEEEEAAAAAANUUUUUUUUTTTT!'
The cry started in the living room and finished, arriving at pace, in the hallway.

'LITTLE-BIT!' replied Peanut as she scooped up her excited younger sister and hugged her. 'What adventures have you had today then?'

The nickname gene was strong in the Jones family. Its youngest member had been born just over five years ago and her parents had named her Elizabeth May. Elizabeth was an unusually early talker, saying her first word ('trousers') when she was just under a year old, but she had always had trouble saying her own name. 'Lilibet' was the closest she could get. Over time (and with the help of her big sister) this became

'Little-Bit'. Needless to say, the nickname stuck.

'Well,' said Little-Bit, 'today at school I was playing in the play kitchen with Marley and Marley said that he wanted to pretend-cook a fried egg in the play kitchen and I said that Marley couldn't pretend-cook a fried egg in the play kitchen because I was using the frying pan to pretend-cook some sausages and then Marley said that he could just use the oven to pretend-cook his fried egg and I said don't be silly Marley you need the hot, flat surface area of the frying pan in order to get the egg's molecules to move as fast as possible so that they collide and weaken the bonds holding the amino acid chains together thus enabling the loose protein strings to move and tangle together turning the liquid egg into a semi-solid state and if you do that in the oven the egg will eventually bake but it will take far too long.' She paused to catch her breath. 'And do you know what Marley did?'

'What did Marley do?' giggled Peanut.

'He went to play dressing-up with Weronika.'

Despite being seven years her senior, Peanut loved hanging out with her little sister. The

combination of Little-Bit being unusually bright and Peanut embracing her inner five-year-old whenever possible meant that they shared exactly the same sense of humour.

Most of their games involved the family pets. For example, Giles the dog would often find himself wearing a cap and a pair of sunglasses, propelling himself along on a skateboard trying to catch the dog biscuit attached to the end of the small fishing rod that was, in turn, attached to his cap.

Their cat, Catface, on the other hand, would regularly find herself wearing a bonnet, sitting in a makeshift cat classroom and being taught her ABCs by Little-Bit. For the entirety of the game, the cat's name would be Jennifer Four-Year-Old. More often than not, Peanut played the part of Lavender Well-To-Do, a classmate of Jennifer's.

'Oh well, it's Marley's loss, I guess,' said Little-Bit. 'What's for dinner, Mummy?'

10
Dinner, Interrupted

'So, why did you do it?' asked Mum in between a mouthful of shepherd's pie and a glug of red wine.

'Why did I do *what*?' said Peanut.

'Why did you deliberately do something that would put you in detention? That's your fourth in three weeks.'

'Oh, that. Well, basically, I keep getting detentions because . . . ALL OF THE TEACHERS AT ST HUBERT'S ARE ABSOLUTE IDIOTS!' Peanut felt herself getting cross at the mere thought of Death Breath.

'Don't raise your voice at me, young lady. I think it's about time you grew up, that's what I think. You can't go around drawing vampire zombies in your exercise books. You're not seven years old!'

'First, I am pretty grown-up, *actually*. Second, it wasn't a vampire zombie, it was a vampire unicorn. And third, why don't you just leave me alone?'

'I agree with Peanut,' said Little-Bit without looking up from her plate of Dino Bites.

'Nobody asked you,' snapped Mum. 'Peanut, I know you have yet to find your feet at St Hubert's, but I expect you to at least put some effort in. Why don't you try to make some friends? That'd be a start, at least.'

A phone started to ring. Mum jumped up from her chair and rummaged through her handbag.

'Oh, where *is* it? Ah, here we go.' She slid her finger across the screen. 'Hello . . . ? Oh, hi, Milton.' She was talking in that strange voice that Peanut didn't recognise. 'Is this about the Globetown report? Is there something else I need to include? Oh . . . Oh, I see. Right. Well, er, that would be . . . lovely. Yes, yes, six thirty tomorrow evening is fine. Yes. Thank you. I'll, er, I'll see you in the morning. OK then. Goodnight.'

Peanut eyed her mum suspiciously. 'Please tell me that what just happened isn't what I think just happened,' she said, a bead of sweat appearing on her forehead.

'Well, that depends on what you think happened, doesn't it? Eat your dinner, Peanut.'

'Oh, it's "Peanut" again, is it? Not *Pernilla*? I wonder what you'll refer to me as tomorrow night on your *date* with Mr Stoneyface Greasyboy!'

'That's enough! Milton has simply invited me to dinner tomorrow night to discuss my career path.' Mum's face flushed. 'There's nothing more to it than that. Leo, will you be able to look after your sisters after the childminder goes home?'

'I guess,' said Leo, shrugging and avoiding eye contact with his mother. They were the first words he'd spoken since they'd been at the table.

'OK!' shouted Peanut. 'Stop the world, I'm getting off!'

'Pardon?' said Mum.

'Have you totally forgotten about Dad? I cannot believe you are going to pretend he never existed and start going out with that horrible man! If Dad was here—'

'Well Dad's not here, is he?' said Mum icily.

'No. He's probably been kidnapped and is being held against his will in some awful dungeon somewhere. Meanwhile, you are totally ignoring it and going out on dates!'

'He has not been kidnapped, Peanut. He left us. He wrote months ago to tell us that he'd left us.'

'He would never do that! You know he'd never do that!' Peanut's voice was cracking.

'You know what? I've just about had enough of answering to a twelve-year-old child. If you don't like it then you can just . . . go to your room.'

'Oh, don't worry. I'm going!'

Peanut stomped out of the dining room, making as much noise with her feet on the stairs as she possibly could. She ran into her bedroom, slammed the door shut behind her and dived on to the bed.

She lay still, breathing deeply as her heart rate gradually slowed and returned to normal. After a few minutes, she rolled across her duvet and reached out to her bedside table for the wooden box full of Post-it notes. She slowly ran her fingers over the letters carved into the lid before she opened it. Looking at the pictures Dad had drawn over the years was always comforting. It made Peanut feel as if he were nearby. He might have written the words 'Love you forever x' on more than 2,000 drawings, but she never tired of reading them.

'I love you too, Dad,' she whispered. 'I'm going to find you. I promise.'

She tipped all of the notes on to her bed and spread them out on the duvet. Mickey Mouse, Paddington Bear, that cute scribbly dog, and hundreds of other familiar faces stared back at her. As Peanut reached over to grab a particularly intricate mini-version of a painting called *The Kiss* by Gustav Klimt, she knocked the empty box with her elbow, and it crashed to the floor.

A shout came from downstairs: 'If you know what's good for you, you'll stop throwing things around your room, young lady!'

Peanut sighed and bent down to pick up the box. As she lifted it back on to the bed, she felt a slight movement within. She looked inside. There was nothing there. She shook it. There it was again. A very faint tapping sound. What could it be? She felt all around the interior, the long sides, the short sides, the bottom. *Ah. A bit of give.* She tried to lever the edges. Nothing. Then she pushed the base with her fingers. Suddenly, something seemed to release, like a push-click cupboard door. It popped open.

The secret compartment was slightly cushioned by a dark-green velvet lining, exactly like the one in Mum's jewellery box. Along the centre ran a long, narrow groove, and sitting snugly in that groove was . . .

. . . a pencil.

11
Little Tail

he pencil was eighteen centimetres long and bright yellow. But it wasn't your usual machine-hewn, perfectly hexagonal cylinder of wood, with a smooth point at one end and an eraser at the other. Oh no. For a start, it looked really old. Like, really, really old. Secondly, it had the feel of an object that had been whittled by hand. Carved, almost. None of the lines was quite straight. It looked more like a sculpture of a pencil than an actual writing implement.

The pointy end, in particular, was quite remarkable. There

was a centimetre or so of bare wood (the yellow coating looked like it had been hacked away by someone with a miniature axe) that surrounded a thick, black lead. The exposed lead was way longer than Peanut was used to: about half the length of her thumb. It too had a handmade feel, extending fairly evenly for a couple of centimetres before suddenly tapering to a very sharp point.

The other end featured a small length of what looked like very thin silver rope that had been wrapped around the pencil six times. It was holding a centimetre of pale blue rubber, roughly cut into a cylindrical shape.

What Peanut was most fascinated by, however, were the faded letters running along the main body of the pencil. They had been printed very unevenly in black, and they read:

L . . . . O R . . . E

All in all, it was, without doubt, the most beautiful object that Peanut had ever seen. Little Tail – that was the name on its box. She stared at it for a good five minutes before she dared pick it up.

When she did, it was heavier than she'd expected. She mimed drawing a few shapes in the air while Catface, who had been hiding in her usual spot underneath the wardrobe, watched with a confused look on her face. Peanut jumped from the bed, rummaged through one of the piles on her desk and pulled out a plain piece of cartridge paper. She thought about how her life had changed since last year and how hopeless she felt. She wished that everything was the way it used to be. What she wouldn't give to wake up in the morning, kiss Mum and Dad goodbye and head off to Melody High.

She recalled something Dad would tell her whenever she felt worried:

'Remember, Peanut, wherever a flower blooms, so does hope. Even the tiniest plant can have the toughest roots.'

She started to draw. The pencil moved across the paper

smoothly, its line crisp and even. It felt perfectly balanced in her hand, almost like it was an extension of her arm. Before she knew it, she was finished. She held up the drawing.

'Wherever a flower blooms, so does hope,' she said aloud.

Catface yawned. Peanut looked over at her and yawned too. She suddenly felt exhausted.

She found some Blu Tack and stuck her drawing to the wall, right next to her favourite Fantastic Four postcard. She carefully laid the pencil back in its secret hiding place in the box, put her pyjamas on and climbed into bed. She was asleep as soon as her head hit the pillow.

12
A Spillage

s usual, Peanut woke up at 6.59 a.m., exactly one minute before her alarm went off. She sat up, stretched, swung her legs out from underneath the duvet and perched herself on the edge of the bed. As she rubbed her eyes, she remembered the argument with Mum the previous evening and felt her shoulders slump.

Then she thought about the beautiful pencil, and her spirits lifted slightly. She glanced up at her drawing from the previous evening. When she saw it, she could not believe her eyes.

'What? No. How?'

The flower that she had drawn . . . had wilted. It was now an illustration of a dead flower in a vase.

A thousand thoughts went through her head at the same time.

'Someone must have broken into my room in the night and changed it!'

'Maybe I'm still asleep and this is a dream.'

'Maybe I imagined the whole thing.'

'Maybe that is what I drew last night after all.'

'Am I going crazy?'

'Aaaaarrrrrgggggh!'

She leaped from the bed and grabbed the piece of paper. As she pulled it from the wall, something even more incredible happened: the vase in the picture fell over and smashed. It *actually* smashed. And what's more, a small puddle of water was spreading across the drawing. There were even some splash marks on her Fantastic Four postcard.

Peanut suddenly felt a bit strange. The blood drained from her face and everything started to turn white. She felt very dizzy. She lay back on the bed and closed her eyes.

A little while later, she opened them, sat up and once again looked at the drawing which was now lying on the

bed next to her. It showed several shards of broken china floating in small puddles of water, and a rather sorry-looking flower lying among them.

'What is going on?' she gasped.

The bedroom door burst open.

'Peanut! Someone called Rockwell arrived five minutes ago,' said Mum. 'He says you arranged to walk to school together. You, meanwhile, have been ignoring me for the past half an hour. You must have overslept. Now get dressed as quickly as you can and I'll give you some fruit to eat on the way to school.'

'Your new friend seems nice, by the way.'

'He's not my friend,' Peanut muttered as she leaped off the bed and started pulling on her school uniform. 'We're just studying together.'

She ran to the bathroom, brushed her teeth, skidded back into her bedroom, opened the wooden box, released the false base, grabbed the pencil, put it in her blazer pocket and thundered down the stairs.

'Sorry,' she said to Rockwell, who was standing in the hallway. 'I overslept. Just grabbing an apple.'

13
Peanut's Weird Story

'So, I thought we could start by going over some basic physics stuff,' said Rockwell, barely able to suppress the excitement in his voice. 'Forces and motion, maybe? Death Breath said he was going to test us tomorrow, and I bet that Newton's Second Law comes up. Must remember that acceleration is *inversely* proportional to mass. I always forget that bit.'

Peanut took a bite of her apple. 'Whatever.'

'OK, what's up?' sighed Rockwell. 'Have you changed your mind about studying together? Do you want me to walk five metres ahead of you as usual?'

'No, it's not that. It's just . . . Oh, never mind.'

'Come on, Peanut. Tell me. That's what friends are for,

after all.'

'We're not friends,' she spluttered, accidentally spraying Rockwell with bits of chewed apple.

'OK,' he replied, wiping his face. 'That's what study buddies are for then.' He smiled, showing a set of perfectly even, white teeth. 'Please . . .'

'All right then, but I'm warning you, it's a bit weird.'

Rockwell swallowed, steeled himself, and said, 'OK. Shoot.'

She told him what had happened the night before. About the argument, the wooden box, the Post-it notes, the pencil and the strange drawing that came to life. It had been a long time since she had shared anything about herself with anybody, and she was surprised at how nice it felt. Also, saying it out loud made it feel real, like it had actually happened.

When she'd finished describing the 'water' splashing on to the Fantastic Four postcard, she stopped and looked at Rockwell.

'You think I've lost the plot, don't you?'

'Nooooooo. Why would I think that?' replied Rockwell. 'If you say that's what you think you saw, then as far as I'm concerned, that's what you think you saw. Er, just out of interest, have you been feeling under the weather recently? Have you maybe eaten anything . . . unusual at all?'

'I don't *think* I saw it, I *did* actually see it,' snapped Peanut. 'See? I knew it was pointless telling you!'

'OK, OK. I'm sorry. So, have you brought this magic pencil with you today?'

'Of course I have. It's in my pocket.'

Rockwell paused to think. 'OK. Well, as Mr Dawkins says, if you really want to see whether something will behave the way you think it is going to behave, you have to conduct a controlled experiment to prove or disprove your hypothesis.'

'Your what?'

'Your hypothesis. It's a theory you can test. In other words, we need to test the pencil.' He reached into the inside pocket of his blazer, pulled out his diary and started flipping through the pages. 'Brilliant! It's SLPC today! Meet me in Lab 3 at twelve thirty.'

'What's SLPC?' asked Peanut.

'Student-Led Physics Club. Don't worry, I'm the only member, so we'll have the lab to ourselves. We'll be able to conduct our little experiment in peace.'

The Experiment

'Do I have to wear these?' Peanut pulled the school-issue plastic safety goggles over her head and let the elastic strap snap against the back of her skull.

'Safety *first* so you *last*,' replied Rockwell, pleased with himself for remembering one of Death Breath's many catchphrases. 'Right, let's do this. Where's this pencil then?'

Peanut pulled it out from her blazer pocket and handed it to Rockwell. He cradled it with both hands as if it were the Elder Wand, and slowly lifted it up towards the light. Peanut thought she could hear the Hallelujah Chorus playing somewhere.

'It's beautiful,' he said in a strange trance-like voice. Then he burst out laughing.

Peanut, who had thought he was being serious, immediately flushed with embarrassment. Rockwell realised that he'd misjudged the situation. 'Actually, I – er – think that maybe y-you should do this. It's your p-pencil after all,' he stammered, handing it back to Peanut.

'Of course I should do this,' harrumphed Peanut. She grabbed the pencil from him and pulled a sketchbook from her rucksack.

She sat at the bench and started to draw. Again, she was struck by the pencil's weight and how easily the lead seemed to glide across the page. It was as smooth as silk. She was so caught up with how nice the pencil felt to hold that she'd almost finished the picture before she realised what it was she was drawing. It was an apple. Exactly like the one she had eaten on the way to school that morning.

Peanut looked at her sketch and smiled. It was good. Better than usual. In fact, she thought, it might be the best drawing she'd ever done. She held the pencil up to her eye, studied the tip, then picked up the sketchbook, turned around and held it up to show Rockwell.

'What do you think?'

'Crikey!' he exclaimed. 'It's brilliant!'

She felt her cheeks redden. 'Thanks.'

She ripped the page out of the sketchbook, grabbed a piece of tape and stuck the drawing to the whiteboard. 'OK,' she said. 'Pick up the apple.'

Rockwell laughed. 'Yeah, right,' he said. But Peanut wasn't smiling. 'Oh. You mean you actually want me to do this?' he said. 'Come on, the joke's over now. If this is your way of trying to make me look like an idiot it's not going to work.'

'Look. You said yourself you have to conduct a controlled experiment to either prove or disprove a hypothesis. Well, my theory is that the stuff I draw with this pencil becomes real. If you're so smart, why don't you prove me wrong?'

Rockwell looked at her. He could tell she was serious. 'OK. You asked for it . . .' he said nervously.

He reached out towards the picture, extending his fingers as if to grab the apple. He glanced over at Peanut and smiled. He looked back at the drawing and took a deep breath.

Then something very strange happened. At the point where Rockwell expected to feel the surface of the paper, he felt . . . nothing. Not a sausage. Nada. In fact, his hand just kept moving. It kept moving *into* the drawing, straight towards the piece of fruit. Two seconds later, to his utter amazement, his fingertips touched the apple. Instinctively, his hand closed around it and then, miracle of miracles, Rockwell pulled Peanut's sketch out of the sheet of paper and held it in his hand.

15
Apple Crumble

ockwell's eyes were so wide open that Peanut thought they might pop out of his head and bounce on to the floor like ping-pong balls.

'So, do you believe me now?' said Peanut.

As soon as she'd said the words, a second very strange thing happened. The drawing of the apple that Rockwell was holding slowly started to crumble. 'What's going on?' Rockwell shrieked as it disintegrated right in front of their eyes. Seconds later, all that was left was a small pile of very fine, silvery grey powder.

Rockwell looked up at Peanut.

He looked down at his hands.

He looked back up at Peanut.

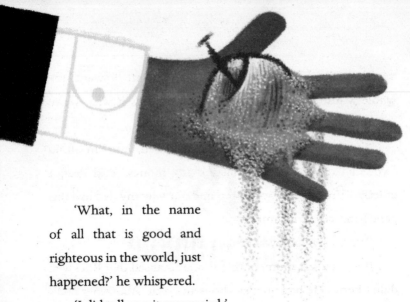

'What, in the name
of all that is good and
righteous in the world, just
happened?' he whispered.

'I did tell you it was weird.'

'Weird? It's flippin' amazing!' he yelled. 'Like something
out of Harry Potter!'

Peanut was taken aback at the size and volume of
Rockwell's reaction.

'OHMYGOD! ACTUAL REAL-LIFE MAGIC! Do you
know what this means? You are going to be sooooooooooooo
rich!' He started dancing around the lab singing something
about it always being sunny in a rich man's world.

When he finally moonwalked back to where she was
standing (and spun around to face her with a loud 'Whoo-
hoo!') she put her finger to her lips.

'Sssshhhhhhhh! Do you want the whole world to know
what we've got here?'

'Er, yes. Yes, I do. In fact, not only do I want the whole

world to know what we've got here, but I want the whole world to give us lots of money to show it what we've got here!'

'I'm sorry to disappoint you, Rockwell, but I'm afraid I couldn't care less about making any money,' said Peanut quietly. 'What I really want is to find out why my dad had this pencil and where it came from.'

'Well, why don't you just ask him?'

It was at that moment that Peanut realised that Rockwell didn't know. He had no idea about any of it. About her dad's strange disappearance, about the police investigation, about her mum going mad and making her change schools. None of it. She hadn't told him about all that stuff because, well, they weren't friends.

'OK. I need to tell you something.' She took a deep breath and, for the second time that day, she found herself confiding in Rockwell.

'Oh, Peanut,' he said when she'd finished. 'I'm so sorry about your dad. I remember how sad I felt when my dad moved out, and he only went to a flat three floors below us in the same block. That was bad enough, so it must be awful not knowing where he's gone.'

Peanut nodded. 'Yes. It is.' A small smile played on her lips. 'Thanks, Rockwell.'

'What for?' He looked confused.

'You're the only person, besides me, who doesn't believe that he ran away to Mexico.'

'Yes, well, you know your dad, right? If you think he disappeared, he disappeared.'

'I do,' she agreed.

'Well, then . . . Hey! You know what I think?' said Rockwell excitedly. 'I think that your dad *wanted* you to find this pencil. I think it's a clue as to what might have happened to him. Can I have a closer look?'

Peanut handed the pencil over to him. 'It has some strange lettering on the side. I think it says "LORE". What does "lore" mean?'

Rockwell pulled a handkerchief from his pocket and carefully wrapped it around the pencil. 'Well, there's only one way to find out.' He picked up his bag. 'Let's go to the library.'

16
Nicolas-Jacques Conté

eanut and Rockwell skidded to a stop in the library's reference section, having run at full speed through the corridors to get there. They had about ten minutes to do their research before the bell went for their next lesson.

'Tell me again: why don't we just google it when we get home?' asked Peanut, mindful of the fact that mobile phones were banned at St Hubert's.

'No time like the present,' replied Rockwell. 'You do want to find your dad, don't you? Anyway, can't you smell it?'

'Smell what? Oh no. You haven't, have you?'

'No!' shouted Rockwell, blushing. 'I mean, can't you smell . . . the knowledge?'

'I don't know about any "knowledge", but I can definitely smell these musty old books. This dictionary must be from the nineties. It's *ancient!*'

'I *love* the smell of libraries,' said Rockwell wistfully. 'All those pages full of facts, opinion and analysis. Don't get me wrong, computers are great and everything, but there is nothing like a bit of analogue action when it comes to learning. One day I'm going to have an entire section in this room dedicated to me and my wisdom. You just wait and see.'

'I'm sure you're right,' said Peanut. 'But in the meantime, let's look up what "LORE" means, shall we?'

She pulled the dictionary from the shelf, blew the dust off the cover, opened it and started flicking through the 'L' section.

'Ah. Here it is!' she shouted.

LORE {lor}
noun

- Collective knowledge or wisdom on a particular subject, especially of a traditional nature
- Knowledge or learning
- Teachings, or something that is taught (archaic)

Knowledge! It says *knowledge!* See? I told you I could smell it,' said Rockwell, smiling.

'I don't understand,' Peanut said. 'What collective

knowledge or wisdom? What teachings? Rockwell? Rockwell?'

He had moved further down the aisle and was leafing through the biggest book that Peanut had ever seen in her life. He was doing his best to turn the pages while he held on to it with both arms. It looked super-heavy.

'Need some help?' asked Peanut.

'Yes please,' puffed Rockwell. 'I thought I'd grab this encyclopaedia and look up who the inventor of the pencil was. See if it tells us anything about ours.'

'That's actually a really good idea,' said Peanut as she helped Rockwell lower the book to the floor. 'Hang on a second. What do you mean, *"ours"*?'

'Right. Let's have a look,' said Rockwell, ignoring her. 'Yes. Here we are. "The History of the Pencil".' His expression intensified as he read the entry.

'Well?' said Peanut impatiently.

'It says here that it was invented by some French bloke called Nicolas-Jacques Conté in the eighteenth century. Basically, the British wouldn't sell France any graphite, so he decided to mix what powdered graphite they had with clay, and make the lead that way. Then he clamped it between two half-cylinders of wood to make the first ever version of the handy drawing implement we all know and love.'

'Hmm, so maybe our pencil is French, then,' mused Peanut.

'Oh, so it is *ours*, then?' said Rockwell, smiling.

DDDRRRRRRRRRRIIIIIIIIIINNNNNNNNGGGGGGG!!

The end-of-lunch bell almost deafened the pair. Rockwell slammed the encyclopaedia shut and heaved it back on to the shelf.

'Gotta run, Peanut! Double chemistry now, and Mrs Bloyce does *not* appreciate lateness.'

'OK. Er, shall we meet at the end of school then and see if we can find out anything else?' asked Peanut.

'Can't. Chess Club. I'll call for you in the morning and we'll work out what to do next. OK?'

'OK. But remember, this doesn't mean—'

'I know, I know,' he said, smiling. 'This doesn't mean we're friends. I'll see you in the morning.'

17
A Little-Bit of Help

'Leighann, I'm home!' shouted Peanut.

'At last!' called a voice from the kitchen. 'Where have you been? It's nearly six o'clock. I was getting worried.'

'Detention, obviously,' she replied. 'I've been doing litter duty for the last two hours.'

Peanut flung her coat over the banister, kicked off her shoes and headed straight into the kitchen looking for snacks. There she found the Joneses' childminder creating some kind of sculptural masterpiece via the medium of Little-Bit's hair.

'You must be starving, sweetie. There's some lasagne in the oven. Help yourself.'

Leighann followed Peanut's gaze to the plait she was weaving. 'It's called a waterfall braid,' she said. Sure enough, her little sister's honey-coloured locks were cascading down to her shoulders from a neat plait that circled the rear of her head. It looked just like a waterfall.

'It's amazing,' said Peanut.

'Thanks, sweetie. Now, don't forget, your mum's going out for dinner with her boss tonight, so Leo's in charge. She came home early from work to get ready,' said Leighann.

'Ugh. How could I forget?' groaned Peanut, before grabbing a cereal bar and a satsuma and heading up to her bedroom, rucksack on her back. 'I'll come down for dinner after she's gone,' she called over her shoulder.

When Peanut opened the door to her room, the first thing she saw was the picture of the broken vase lying on her bed. She raced over, picked it up and carefully put it on her desk. She took the pencil, still swaddled in Rockwell's handkerchief, from her blazer pocket, unwrapped it and placed it next to the drawing. Then she picked up one of her many sketchbooks, found a blank page and wrote 'LORE' in big block letters (with a rather fetching three-dimensional bevel effect).

She stared at the sketchbook. What could it mean? Is it an anagram? She started scribbling more words:

ROLE ORLE ERLO
RELO LERO

She scratched her head. She wasn't getting anywhere. Then, suddenly, the door crashed open.

'PEEEEEEEAAAAANNNNNUUUUUUUTTTTTT!'

Peanut spun around as Little-Bit came hurtling into the room, hair waterfall flying through the air behind her, just in time to catch her in a big hug.

'Hi, LB!'

'Whatchya doing?' Little-Bit asked. She was looking at the open sketchbook on the desk behind Peanut.

'Oh. Just trying to work something out.'

'Are you trying to work out which letters are missing on your new pencil?' said Little-Bit, picking it up from next to the sketchbook.

'Be careful with that,' said Peanut. 'Anyway, what do you mean, "missing"?'

'Oh, it's just that it looks a bit like one of those missing letter games, the ones in my *Junior Puzzler Compendium*.'

'Missing letters? But there *are* letters there. L, O, R and E.'

'Yes, but I've immediately noticed two things about those.

First, they are only just visible. The R, for example, has almost disappeared. Like it's been rubbed off. And second, the spacing between the letters is very uneven. That, to me, is suspicious. If the R can be rubbed off, then so can other letters that might once have been in those spaces. I think that's what's happened here. We have a missing letters puzzle.'

Sometimes, having a younger sister who is clearly smarter than you are could be really annoying. This was *not* one of those times.

'Little-Bit, you're a *genius!*' shouted Peanut, and she gave her sister a big kiss on the cheek.

Downstairs, the doorbell rang.

'I'll get it!' shouted Mum, and the girls heard her clumping down the stairs in her high heels.

'Good evening, Tracey darling. Long time no see. Ha ha.'

The sound of Mr Stone's voice smarming up to her mum made Peanut feel ill.

'Bye, kids. Bye, Leighann. Don't go to bed too late, guys.' shouted Mum. The door slammed shut.

'Little-Bit! Get your PJs on!' yelled Leighann up the stairs. 'I have to head home soon.'

'You'd better go,' said Peanut. 'I don't want you getting in trouble too! I'll let you know if I solve the puzzle in the morning.'

'Promise?' said Little-Bit.

'Promise,' said Peanut.

18.
The Door

eanut wrote the letters down again, this time leaving spaces exactly as they appeared on the pencil.

L__OR_E

She tried for an hour, testing every combination of letters she could think of, but she couldn't find a single word that would fit.

She started to think about the research that she'd done with Rockwell in the library. 'Collective knowledge or wisdom'. 'Teachings'.

'OK. If I had invented this magic pencil, what would I write on it?' she said to nobody in particular.

Suddenly, something in that sentence triggered a brainwave. 'If *I* had invented the pencil,' she muttered. She hadn't invented this pencil, or any other pencil, but as they'd discovered earlier, Nicolas-Jacques Conté had, and he was . . . FRENCH!

'It's a French word!!' she shouted.

She looked back down at the puzzle and suddenly saw things more clearly.

Well, it's bound to start with a 'le' or a 'la', she thought. As far as Peanut could remember, nearly all French words did. So she started to fill in the gaps.

$$L(E \text{ or } A)\_OR\_E$$

Then she had one of those rare moments of clarity that only come along once in a blue moon. Remembering a particularly fun French vocab lesson from last year at Melody High, she picked up the pencil and wrote . . .

$$LAPORTE$$

'*La Porte*,' she whispered. 'French for "The Door". Maybe this pencil is actually a key . . .'

Then, yet another idea popped into her head. 'Surely that wouldn't work. Would it?'

Peanut jumped from the chair, ran over to her wardrobe and pulled out a big roll of paper. She unfurled it on the floor, picked up the yellow pencil and started to draw.

When she had finished, she picked the piece of paper up, grabbed some Blu Tack and stuck it to the wardrobe door.

She stepped back and looked at her drawing. It was pretty good, even if she did say so herself. Quickly she pulled on a dressing gown and her school shoes, checked the time (8.01 p.m.), tucked the pencil behind her ear and focused on the sketch of the doorknob.

Taking a deep breath, she held out her hand, reached into the picture and grabbed the knob. It felt cold, as if it were made of brass rather than graphite. Peanut rotated it a quarter turn anti-clockwise. Something clicked.

And then the door opened . . .

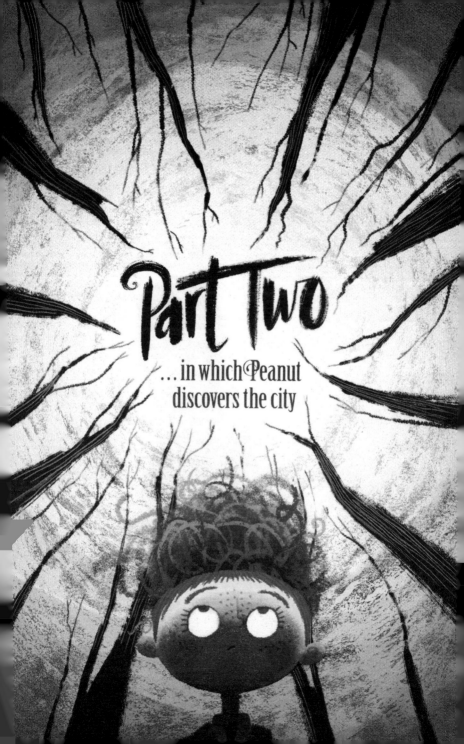

Part Two

…in which Peanut
discovers the city

19
Chroma

Nervously Peanut stepped through the door and closed it behind her.

A wave of freezing cold air hit hard as her eyes struggled to adapt to the brightness. When they eventually began to adjust, she saw that she was standing alone in a vast, snow-covered landscape. It was hard to tell where the ground ended and the sky began. Everything was completely white except for a few jagged trees that punched through the snow like spiky, black fingers clawing at the heavens. They looked like they had been drawn very quickly with a piece of charcoal.

Peanut tightened her dressing-gown cord and started to trudge through the ankle-deep snow.

After a minute or two, she glanced back over her shoulder

and was relieved to see that the door hadn't crumbled away to a fine, silvery grey powder, like the apple she'd drawn earlier that day. Maybe the magic worked differently because she was inside the drawing? she wondered. But was she *inside* it, or had she gone through the picture to another place entirely? Then something else caught her eye just beyond the door. She started to walk back. As she got closer, she saw two signposts, one short and wide, and one tall and thin. They too looked like drawings. She broke into a jog.

She got to the shorter one first.

The other sign was much taller, about half the height of her house on Melody Road. It consisted of a thick central pole with lots of flat, arrow-shaped arms coming off of it, all pointing in different directions. Each arm had words painted on it. Peanut read a few. 'Ink District', 'Warholia', 'The Strip'. At the very top was a much larger panel sporting the words 'You are in The North Draw'.

YOU ARE IN
THE NORTH D...

VINCENT FIELDS

CUBESIDE

THE STRIP

DALI POINT WEST

INK DISTRICT

GOBERNIA

THE GRID

EIGHT DISTRICT

WARHOLIA

As she was deciding which arrow to follow, she noticed some small pawprints in the snow by the base. They looked just like the ones that Giles often left in the kitchen after a walk in the Great Woods. Instinctively she started to follow them.

They led down through the valley from a ridge in the distance, before passing the signpost and continuing towards a small cluster of charcoal-coloured trees. As she got closer to the trees, she thought she could hear something. Maybe it was just the wind? She reached the first tree and leaned on the trunk. It felt strangely dusty and left a thin layer of black powder on her hand. She wiped it on her dressing gown and held her breath to listen. Yes. There it was. And again. A soft crying sound. A whimper, almost. There was definitely something in among the trees, and that something was definitely alive.

Peanut swallowed hard and headed into the copse.

Treading as quietly as possible, she moved slowly. The footprints zigged and zagged before disappearing around the back of the largest tree.

Nervously Peanut poked her head around the trunk.

Sitting there was a small dog. Or at least a sketch of one. A scribble of fur with legs and a tail. Even though he was unlike any dog Peanut had ever seen before, there was something about him that felt . . . familiar.

He was shivering. He looked up at Peanut with big, inky eyes and his tail to started to wag.

'Hello, boy. What are you doing out here all on your own? You must be freezing.'

She ruffled the fur around his neck with both hands. Considering the dog was made entirely of pencil lead and ink, he was very soft and *very* fluffy. She felt for his collar and traced around it with her hands until she found the tag.

'The Markmakers? Who or what are the Markmakers?'

Doodle stood up and wagged his tail faster.

'Hmmm. Let's see if we can get you home, shall we?'

Peanut retraced her steps through the trees and back

out into the open. Nothing. Certainly no sign of a house. Doodle, meanwhile, started to circle her feet and bark, tail wagging furiously.

'Oh, you want to play, do you?' said Peanut. She looked around for a stick to throw, but the charcoal trees didn't seem to have dropped any of their branches. Then she had an idea. She pulled the pencil from behind her ear.

'I wonder,' she said. 'OK, now focus, Peanut . . .'

She imagined there was a big piece of paper on an invisible easel in front of her. She held the pencil in her left hand, raised it up to shoulder height and started to draw in the air. To her amazement, a dark grey line appeared from the tip of the lead.

She gasped and dropped the pencil, but the line stayed exactly where it was, just . . . hovering. She took a deep breath, picked up the pencil and tried something else. This time she drew a ball.

When she was done, she reached out towards the picture and felt a frisson of excitement as her fingers closed around it. It felt like, well, a ball. Solid and heavy.

'WOOF! WOOF!'

Doodle was still at her feet, looking up keenly at the object in Peanut's hand.

'WOOF!'

Peanut threw it as far as she could, and sure enough, the dog galloped across the snow in hot pursuit. He grabbed it and

brought it back, dropping it at her feet.

'Clever boy!'

They carried on playing fetch as the light faded, until her arm started to get tired, at which point she decided to try something different. She took the pencil and drafted a sketch of a simple catapult. She plucked it from the air, placed the ball in the cradle and pulled it back slowly. Doodle started to bark. When the elastic was stretched as tightly as possible, she let go. The ball flew from the sling-shot like a bullet and the dog immediately sprinted after it. Peanut watched as it traced a high arc through the night sky before landing in the snow a couple of hundred metres away.

When he was halfway to the ball, Doodle suddenly stopped dead. He stared ahead for a few seconds, then turned around, tail between his legs, and walked back to Peanut.

'What's wrong, Doodle? Are you scared of something? It's OK, boy. There's nothing there. Don't worry.'

Peanut reached down to stroke him and as she did so she caught a glimpse of her watch.

'Oh no! Mum's going to kill me!'

20
Bye-Bye, Boy

Peanut ruffled Doodle's scribbly fur. 'Bye-bye, boy. I'll be back soon, I promise.'

The dog cocked his head to one side and watched as Peanut ran back towards the door. She grabbed the knob, pulled it open and dived through. As she landed on her bedroom carpet the door slammed shut behind her. Peanut looked back just in time to see it slowly crumble and fall from the roll of paper, leaving a small pile of grey dust on the floor.

She stood up, took her dressing gown off and started to mentally prepare for the inevitable roasting from Mum, who must be back from her date by now. Peanut left her room and headed downstairs.

Unsurprisingly, the lights were all still on. Peanut wondered whether the police would be there yet. Knowing her mother, they probably would. She remembered the time she and Little-Bit had arrived home after taking Giles for a walk to find six police cars parked at strange angles outside their house. They had only taken twenty minutes longer than usual (Little-Bit thought it would be a fun experiment to let the dog escape in order to find out if the microchip embedded in his neck actually worked) and Mum had filed a missing person's report.

Peanut steeled herself and went into the kitchen but, to her relief, there were no police officers there. In fact, there wasn't even a mum! Just Leo, who was slowly loading the dishwasher while wearing his headphones.

'Er, Leo. Why are you still up?' she asked.

Leo pulled a headphone bud from his ear. 'Probably because I'm not six years old.'

'What do you mean? What time is it?'

She looked at her watch.

'WHAT THE—?' she shrieked. How could she have only been gone for nine minutes?

'Something wrong?' said Leo, his tired eyes flashing with anxiety.

'Oh. Er, no. It's nothing. Don't worry about it,' stammered Peanut. 'Actually, I'm really tired. I might just head up to bed.'

Peanut went back upstairs, brushed her teeth and put on her pyjamas. As she climbed into bed, she thought about Doodle all alone in the snow. She imagined him curled up at the base of a tree, frightened, trying to keep warm, and she felt guilty. Something had scared him. Maybe she should have brought him back with her. No, that wouldn't have worked – remember what happened to the door. The idea of Doodle turning into a pile of grey powder didn't bear thinking about.

She grabbed her discarded dressing gown, reached into the pocket and took out the pencil. Then she picked up the wooden box from her bedside table ready to stash Little Tail safely in its hiding place, but as she opened the lid, one of the Post-it notes caught her eye. Suddenly she sat bolt upright in bed and stared at the drawing.

'No way!' she gasped. 'I *knew* he looked familiar!'

On the Post-it was a picture of a dog. A scribble of fur with legs and a tail. He was standing on a snowy hillside next to a tall signpost with lots of flat, arrow-shaped arms coming off of it, all pointing in different directions. Coming out of the dog's mouth was a little speech bubble, inside which was written, 'Hi Peanut!'

'It's Doodle,' she whispered. 'It's *definitely* Doodle. And that's *definitely* the signpost that says "You are in The North Draw" at the top.'

She stood up as the enormity of what this meant began to sink in: not only must her dad have visited Chroma, but he must have met Doodle too – and maybe the Markmakers. Perhaps the answer to why he'd disappeared was in Chroma!

She grabbed a strip of passport photographs of her and Dad pulling funny faces from her pinboard. It was at that moment that Peanut made the decision that would change her life forever.

She spoke directly to the photographs. 'Tomorrow, I'm going to go back to Chroma. I'm going to find out who these Markmakers are and I'm going to take Doodle back to them . . .'

She took a deep breath.

'. . . and then I'm going to ask them if they've seen you.'

She kissed the picture.

'Don't worry, Dad. I'm coming to find you.'

21
The Bandolier

Peanut woke at 6.59 a.m. and jumped straight out of bed. She had lain awake half the night formulating a plan and it was time to put it into action.

She picked up her dressing gown from the floor and removed the thick cord from the belt loops. Then she dug out Granny's old sewing box, threaded a needle with some thick cotton and sewed the two ends of the cord together. Next, she cut several rectangles of differing sizes from the main body of the dressing gown, and stitched them on to the towelling loop. She then put her right arm through it and pulled the whole thing over her head, so that it hung down diagonally across her body like a bandolier.

Finally, she loaded it up with a carefully chosen selection

of art materials: a big block of charcoal, three permanent markers of varying thicknesses, a brush pen, two paintbrushes, a small tin of watercolours, a can of spray paint and, of course, the yellow pencil. On the back, she attached four empty water bottles that she'd fished out of the recycling bin. Then she picked up the strip of passport photos of her and her dad, folded it in half and put it in the front pocket of her dungarees.

She looked in the mirror and nodded.

'OK. I'm ready.'

'PEANUT!' came a cry from downstairs. 'I HAVE TO GO TO WORK EARLY. CAN YOU DROP LITTLE-BIT AT SCHOOL ON YOUR WAY TO ST HUBERT'S PLEASE? OH, AND YOUR FRIEND ROCKWELL IS HERE AGAIN.'

'OK, MUM. I'LL BE DOWN IN A SECOND.'

Quickly Peanut grabbed the sewing box, the scissors and what was left of the dressing gown and stuffed them all into her wardrobe. Just as she was pulling the bandolier off over her head, the door opened and Rockwell walked in.

'Your mum said I could come up. Hope you don't mi— What is *that*?!'

Peanut sighed. 'OK, OK. There have been a few, um, developments. I think you'd better sit down.'

And for the third time in twenty-four hours, she told him everything.

22
La Porte

o, let me get this straight,' said Rockwell, 'You are planning to go back to this "land" –' he made quotation marks with his fingers as he said the last word – 'find this "dog" –' again, quotation marks – 'and then return him to his owners, whose whereabouts are currently totally and utterly unknown to you?'

'Yes.'

'And then you are going to ask them if they have seen your father running around somewhere in this land of make-believe?'

'Yes.'

'And even if this takes you an entire day, that doesn't matter cos time moves much more slowly in this new world, and so you won't be late for school whatever happens?'

'Yes.'

'And all the time that you are on this quest, you are going to be wearing your homemade utility belt and looking like a cross between Vincent Van Gogh and Chewbacca the Wookiee.

'. . .'

'You know, the famous artist who cut off his own ear and the tall, hairy character from *Star Wars*.'

'Of course I know! And yes, I am going to be wearing my bandolier.'

'Oh, well that's fine then. A perfectly normal thing to do on a Thursday morning before school.'

'You don't fancy coming with me then?' She was surprised to discover that the thought of Rockwell helping her on the search was not an entirely unpleasant one.

'Look,' said Rockwell. 'I admit that what happened in the lab yesterday was kind of amazing.'

Peanut arched an eyebrow.

'OK, it was incredible!' He loosened his tie. 'But if you expect me to believe that there is an entire illustrated *world* that exists in parallel to ours, then I'm afraid you are going to be severely disappointed.'

'So do you think I'm making it up?'

'I think that lots of very strange things happened

yesterday, and it's only natural that you should have lots of very strange dreams as a result.' He stood up and placed his thumbs under his lapels as if he were holding a pair of invisible braces. 'I think it was Freud that put forward the notion that the motivation behind *all* dreams is wish-fulfilment, and that the vast majority of dreams occur because of something that happened during the preceding day. "Day Residue" he called it. And I think it was Jung who said that—'

'All right, all right. Give it a rest, Google boy.' Peanut stood up and pulled the yellow pencil from the bandolier. 'I think it's time for another one of your controlled experiments.'

She walked over to the large roll of paper Blu-Tacked to the wardrobe and drew a picture of a door on it, exactly as she had done the night before. She glanced over at Rockwell, before reaching into the drawing and grabbing the handle. He had a nervous expression. As she turned it, there was a clicking sound and the door opened. Immediately, a strong blast of cold air blew into the room, sending pieces of paper flying in all directions.

Rockwell looked stunned. 'Peanut. I will never doubt you again.'

'Sure you won't,' she scoffed. 'Come on then, before my room gets even more trashed than it already is.'

And with that, they walked through the door and closed it behind them.

As the last piece of paper gently floated to the carpet, Little-Bit Jones tiptoed into the bedroom. She walked over to the drawing of the door, reached in and opened it.

23
The North Draw

elcome . . .' trumpeted Peanut, '. . . to The North Draw, Chroma!'

They stood looking out over the undulating, snowy plains.

'It's so beautiful,' said Rockwell.

'It certainly is,' agreed Peanut. 'It looks just like—'

She was interrupted by the sound of the door behind them opening and closing. They spun around to see Little-Bit standing there in her school uniform.

'PEEEEEEAAAAAANNNNNNNNUUUUTTTTTTTTT!'

She ran up to her sister and threw her arms around her.

'Little-Bit! What are you doing here?'

'I heard you talking about another world and that Daddy might be in it and I wanted to see it. To see him. Let me come with you. Pleeeeease.'

'We should take her back,' said Rockwell.

Little-Bit fixed Rockwell with a steely look over Peanut's shoulder. 'Is he your boyfriend?'

'No!' snapped Peanut. 'He's my . . . He's my . . . study buddy.'

'I bet he wants to be your boyfriend.'

'I do not!' squeaked Rockwell, his voice at least three octaves higher than usual. 'Peanut, I really think we should take her back right now.'

'I WANT TO STAY!'

'He's right, LB.'

'Pleeeeease, Peanut. I won't stay for long. Just let me explore with you for a little while.'

'She might actually be able to help,' said Peanut, looking at Rockwell. 'She's the smartest five-year-old I've ever met.'

'*Of course* she is.' He shook his head slowly.

'OK, Little-Bit,' said Peanut, 'You can stay for now. But only till we find Doodle's owners, then you have to go straight home.'

Rockwell looked heavenwards. Little-Bit stuck her tongue out at him over Peanut's shoulder.

'So,' said the little girl, 'who's Doodle?'

At that moment, a small dog exploded out of the group of trees just ahead of them and bounded towards Peanut.

'This –' Peanut laughed – 'is Doodle.'

He jumped into her arms and started licking her face.

'Aw, he's so cute!' Little-Bit giggled.

'He is rather adorable,' agreed Rockwell. 'And he appears to be . . . a drawing. A living, breathing drawing.'

Before they had a chance to stroke him, he jumped from Peanut's arms, barked twice and turned several circles in front of her. He then sprinted off past the copse before stopping, looking back and barking again.

'I think he wants us to follow him,' said Rockwell.

'Hang on a second,' said Peanut. I'm just going to rub the door out. We don't want anybody else following us, do we?'

'Wait!' shouted Rockwell. 'How can you be sure that a new door will take us back to your room and not some other kid's?'

Peanut paused. He was right.

'OK. Time for another one of your controlled tests,' she said, before quickly drawing a new door next to the existing one. When she'd finished, she opened it and peeked through. 'Yup. It's definitely my room.'

Rockwell nodded as she shut the door and proceeded to rub them both out with the pencil's eraser.

When Peanut had finished, they started to walk towards the dog and, sure enough, when they got to within five metres of him, he ran ahead, turned to face them again, and barked.

'Where are you taking us?' whispered Peanut.

The dog led them across the valley, up the other side, and around a small peak. As they turned the corner, they saw a thin plume of pencil-dust smoke coming from a tree stump on the side of the hill. Doodle ran towards it. As they got closer, they realised that the stump was actually a small chimney. Next to it was a large, heavy-looking metal ring attached to a small backplate embedded in the snow.

Doodle stood above it and barked three times.

They heard the sound of approaching footsteps beneath the ground and then, to their surprise, a giant trapdoor opened in the snow. A woman's head appeared, her white hair piled up into a neat bun with two very old-looking pencils, one pink and one blue, sticking out of it. She smiled broadly.

'Hello, young strangers!' she beamed. 'What are you doing all the way out here? Quick! Come in, before they see you.'

24
The Bunker

Peanut, Rockwell and Little-Bit followed the woman and Doodle through the hatch and down a steep flight of stairs. They led to a large, circular room illuminated by a roaring fire at the far end and several flaming torches attached to the walls. Peanut felt as if she were standing in an oil painting. Everywhere she looked, she could see brush marks. In the grain of the floorboards, running through the patterns on the cushions, in the flickering light of the fire. The whole place was slightly ramshackle. It felt as though it had been built, or painted, by someone who was making it up as they went along, which gave the room a lived-in, cosy feel. Peanut loved it.

'Welcome to the Bunker. Please take a seat and make

yourselves comfortable.' Doodle ran over to a small bowl with his name painted on it and started drinking. 'Now then, I'm sure you could use a drop of hot chocolate to warm you up.'

Peanut noticed the lady's eyes flick to the bandolier before she disappeared through a triangular-shaped door. She returned a couple of minutes later holding a tray loaded with steaming mugs.

'Oh my goodness, I have totally forgotten my manners,' she said as she handed out the drinks. 'I should introduce myself. My name is Millicent Markmaker, but that's a bit of a mouthful. You can call me "Mrs M". And it looks like you've already met my dog, Doodle.'

'Ah, so *you're* one of the Markmakers,' said Peanut. 'I'm so glad we found you. I'm Peanut Jones, and these two are

Rockwell and Little-Bit. We need your help.'

'Really?' she said thoughtfully. 'That's a coincidence, because I could do with a bit of help too.'

'You need *our* help?'

'Yes, I think that maybe I do. But I'll get to that in a minute.' Mrs M sat down in a large, beautifully painted red leather armchair and took a sip of tea. 'First, tell me, how did three children find their way here?'

'We don't know,' said Rockwell. 'We're not even sure where "here" is.'

'Hmmm, interesting.' Mrs M's eyes narrowed. 'So you don't actually know where you are?'

'I do! I do!' shouted Little-Bit, who loved nothing more than answering questions. 'Chroma! I saw a sign by that door we came through.'

Mrs M frowned slightly. 'A sign by the, er, door, eh? Well, you are correct, Little-Bit. You *are* in Chroma. But do you know what Chroma is?'

'The weirdest place on Earth?' said Rockwell.

'Ha. Quite possibly,' said Mrs M. 'But it is more commonly known by another name.'

'And what's that?'

'Why, the Illustrated City, of course.'

25.
The Illustrated City

'The Illustrated City?' gasped Peanut. 'So I was right. Everything here has been . . . drawn by somebody.'

'At some point, yes.'

'So who did all of the drawing?' asked Rockwell, wiping hot chocolate from his top lip. 'Whoever it was must have been pretty handy with the old pencils.'

'Ah, now there's a question' replied the old lady. 'The answer is . . . a great many people. Thousands and thousands.'

She put down her mug, stood up and walked over to one of the slightly skew-whiff bookshelves. She started peering at the spines of the books.

'Chroma has been around for as long as anyone can remember. Longer, actually. The history books tell us that it began as a small settlement on a tiny island, and that it has grown over the centuries. It really is quite big now.'

'If it's so big, how come I've never seen it in my junior atlas?' said Little-Bit. 'Or on Mummy's globe in the living room? Or on Google Earth?'

'Ah well, you won't find it on any of your maps, I'm afraid. You see, Chroma is a very special place and only a few very special people from your world ever get to come here.'

'What's so special about us, then?' asked Rockwell.

Mrs M's eyes narrowed. 'That remains to be seen.' She pulled a large book bound in green leather from the shelf and returned to her armchair.

'First, let me tell you a bit about our city. As I said, it all started on an island in the centre of a circular lake. And that lake is where all of the magic comes from.'

'Magic?' said Peanut. 'What magic?'

'Ah. Now we get to the nub of it,' said the old lady, smiling. 'You see, to put it as simply as possible, Chroma is the place where the world's creative and artistic energy comes from. All of it. If Chroma didn't exist, planet Earth would be a pretty colourless, soulless place. The source of all artistic creativity – in your world and mine – is right here, in this city. Specifically, in the Rainbow Lake.'

She opened the book and slid a large piece of folded paper from a pocket on the inside cover.

'It is said that when the original inhabitants swam in the Rainbow Lake, they were suddenly overcome with the urge to create. To draw, to paint, to sculpt, to make. And they found, to their amazement, that whatever they created, even if it was just a flat drawing, became real. If they painted a loaf of bread, they could pick that bread up and eat it. If they drew a horse, they could sit on its back and ride it. The water from the Rainbow Lake made everything that they could possibly imagine real. So almost immediately they started to generate houses, streets, factories, trees, rivers, fields. Very quickly, the city started to expand, and right at its heart, on the island itself, one very special building was erected – a huge, multicoloured tower, over five hundred metres tall. It was, and is, called the Spire.'

'I want to swim in the Rainbow Lake!' shouted Little-Bit.

Mrs M grinned. 'Obviously, as the city grew, so did the population.' She started to unfold the piece of paper. 'It became a thriving hub of beauty and creativity as more and more people contributed to its good looks.'

'You said only a few very special people from our world get to come. So we aren't the first outsiders to travel here, then?' said Peanut, leaning forward.

'Far from it. Nobody is quite sure how they got here – there was a rumour about hidden portals, something like that – but the visitors always kept their secrets and nothing was ever found.' Mrs M stood up and spread the paper on the table in front of them. It was a map. 'Many, if not all, of the most celebrated creatives from your world have spent time in Chroma. Some have even had districts named after them.' She pointed at the piece of paper. 'This should give you an idea of how big the Illustrated City is.'

The three children looked at the map. Peanut recognised lots of the names from the tall signpost.

Mrs M folded her arms. 'So there you have it. One city, three regions, twelve districts. And we –' she tapped a bony finger near the top of the map – 'are right here.'

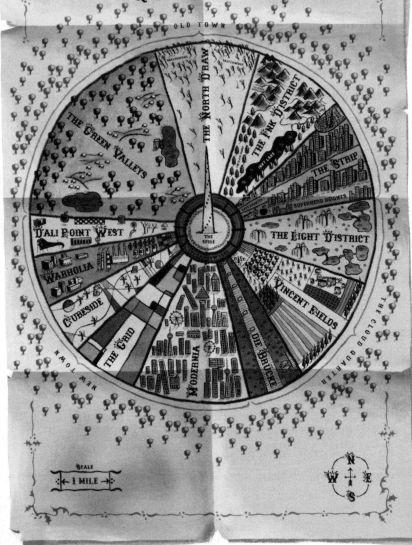

CHROMA
CITY OF COLOUR
& CREATIVITY

26
Mr M

WOOF! WOOF!

'Oh, I'm sorry, Doodle, I forgot to get you some food.' Mrs M went back into the kitchen.

Peanut picked up a small, gilt-framed photograph from the table.

'Pardon me, Mrs M, but who's this standing next to you in the photo?'

There was no reply.

'Mrs M?'

The old lady came back into the room

carrying a bowl of pastel dog biscuits, tears welling in her eyes.

'That's my husband, Malcolm.' She pulled a handkerchief from her sleeve and dabbed her cheeks.

'Ah, yes. I was wondering if there was a Mr M,' said Rockwell. 'So where is he? Is he at work or is he . . . Oh.' His face fell. 'Is Malcolm . . . ? I mean, did he . . . ?'

'As far as I know, he's still alive.' She sniffed. 'Although we haven't had any news for a while.'

'Well, if he's not dead, then where is he?' said Little-Bit, who was kneeling on the floor stroking Doodle as he ate.

'He was taken.'

'Taken?' gasped Peanut. 'Taken by who?'

'By *whom*,' said Rockwell. Peanut shot him daggers.

'A squadron of RAZERs came for him two months ago. On the orders of Mr White.'

'Whoa there, neddy! Let's back up a second, shall we?' said Rockwell, 'RAZERs? Mr White? This is getting confusing. You're going to have to explain.'

Mrs M shook her head as she picked up the photograph of her husband. 'Mr White is a tyrant who won't rest until he has completely destroyed every scrap of creativity and beauty in Chroma. And if he succeeds, it won't just affect us. Your world will completely lose its imaginative spark too. It's because of him that we had to build this bunker in the first place and stay hidden away. Out of sight.' Mrs M's voice was trembling. 'He is the reason that we had to set up the Resistance.'

'The Resistance?'

'Yes. A top secret organisation of people who aren't prepared to let Mr White get away with his terrible plan. We have members all across Chroma, secretly risking their freedom, risking their *lives* to stop him. But it's not easy. Malcolm is the leader of the Resistance and he was captured and imprisoned two months ago. White has the ability to track and monitor every single citizen of Chroma, which makes it almost impossible for anyone to get in and out of his stronghold to rescue Malcolm.'

'I don't understand,' said Little-Bit. 'Who is this Mr White anyway? Why is he in charge? Is he your teacher or something?'

'No, little one. Mr White is the Mayor of Chroma.'

27
Mr White and the RAZERs

Mrs M started collecting up the empty mugs.

'When Mr White first arrived all those years ago, he promised that he would make our fabulous city even better than it already was.'

She laughed in that way that people do when they don't find something funny.

'He told us that if we voted him into power, he would make sure that everyone in Chroma would get the chance to fulfil their creative potential.' She started loading the tray. 'The Rainbow Lake would be colour-corrected twice a week, the Cloud Quarter would be fully solar-powered within a year, and stunning new art galleries would be opened within a decade. The list of promises he made us was endless.'

She took Peanut's mug from her. 'He was also full of warnings about some kind of pollution that was blighting your world, and how, if we weren't careful, it would soon spread to Chroma. He said he knew how to prevent that from happening and if he was elected he would stop it in its tracks.'

She'd stopped collecting the mugs and sat down, staring into the fireplace. 'And do you know what the worst part of this whole sorry affair is?'

The children shook their heads.

'We believed him.' Her eyes shone in the flickering light. 'We should have known straight away that he wouldn't be true to his word. The day after he was elected, he ordered his RAZERs to remove all of the graffiti on Main Street, Warholia.' She looked down and shook her head. 'All that beautiful work. Whitewashed.'

'Er, Mrs M. Sorry to ask, but what *is* a RAZER?' asked Peanut.

'R, A, Z, E, R. Rigorous Attitude Zero Empathy Robot. That should tell you all you need to know. He had them designed and built, and now has hundreds doing his bidding.'

'Yuck. They sound *horrid*,' said Little-Bit. Doodle barked his agreement.

'Finally, after three years of chipping away at everything we held dear, he passed a law making all artistic apparatus illegal. Pens, pencils, pastels, crayons, paintbrushes, everything.

Forbidden. Imagine that. It was all confiscated and impounded. Well, *almost* all of it.' She pointed to the pencils in her hair bun. 'I managed to smuggle these two out when we made our escape underground. They have proved invaluable to our cause over the years.'

'The last straw was when, five years into his mayorship, he painted our beloved Spire white and turned it into a prison. That's when we realised that he wouldn't rest until he had completely destroyed everything that has made this city so great.'

She pulled one of the pencils from her bun, grabbed the map and underlined two words in the title.

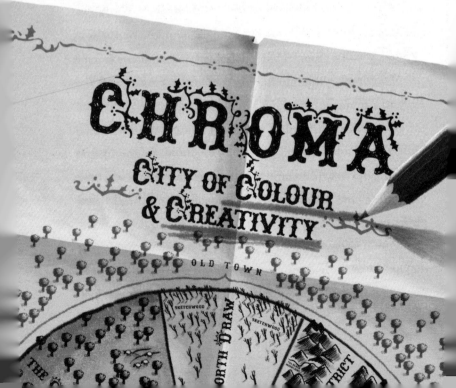

CHROMA
CITY OF COLOUR
& CREATIVITY

OLD TOWN

28
The Big X

'So Mr Markmaker has been taken to the Spire?' said Peanut.

'Yes, my dear. Anyone who disagrees with Mr White can expect a lengthy stay. There are more than a thousand cells, most of which are occupied.'

'Are you *sure* that's where he is?'

'Yes. That's what our intelligence is telling us.' She looked across at the empty armchair next to her own and her eyes filled with tears. 'Sometimes I wonder if I will ever see him again.'

Peanut took Mrs M's hand in hers. Her skin felt like paper. 'What can we do to help?' Peanut asked gently.

Suddenly Little-Bit leaped on to the table, put her fists

on her hips and assumed her best superhero stance. 'DON'T WORRY, MRS M! OUR MISSION IS CLEAR: FIRST, WE SHALL RESCUE MR M! SECOND, WE SHALL DESTROY MR WHITE!'

'Ooh, do be careful up there, little one,' smiled Mrs M. 'I don't want you to take a nasty tumble.'

Peanut lifted Little-Bit off the table. 'The question is, what use could three kids be in the face of a megalomaniac and his army of terrifying robots?'

'Er, did I mention the Big X?' said Mrs M, sounding a tiny bit too casual. 'His most powerful weapon? You'd have to face that too.'

'Th-the Big X. Now, that doesn't sound good,' said Rockwell nervously.

'No. It's not good,' said Mrs M. 'Not good at all.'

'What is the Big X?' asked Peanut.

'Well, imagine the biggest tank that you've ever seen . . .'

'OK.'

'Now quadruple its size . . .'

'OK.'

'Now add a huge set of the sharpest, fastest rotating blades the world has ever known at the front . . .'

'OK.'

'And a huge vent that spits out whatever has been chomped by the blades in the form of greyish, black dust at the back.'

'OK.'

'Well, that's the Big X.'

'Oh.'

'Mr White wants to use the Big X to mono the whole of Chroma.'

'Mono?'

'Yes. Eat up its colour and spit it out. It's his latest initiative. He's already tested it on an entire district.'

'Where did he test it?' Peanut had a nasty feeling that she already knew the answer to her question.

'Right here. In the North Draw. That's why it's so bleak.' Mrs M sighed. 'I wish you could see how it used to be. Full of colour. Full of life . . .' She closed her eyes and smiled. 'It's now barely a sketch of what it used to be.'

Doodle wandered over and jumped up on to Mrs M's lap. She gave him a rub behind his ears. 'Poor old Doodle here was almost caught by the Big X as it ploughed its way through the district. It terrified him. He didn't want to go outside for weeks afterwards and there are still certain areas of the North Draw that he won't set foot in.'

Rockwell stood up, looking very nervous. Peanut realised that he'd been unusually quiet for a long time. 'Er, I th-think it's time we headed back home, actually. I've got triple maths this morning and I've just remembered that I need to brush up on my differentiation before class. It was lovely to meet you, Mrs M. You too, Doodle. But, er, we'd best be off.'

'Sit down, Rockwell,' commanded Little-Bit. He sat down.

'So, how can we help?' asked Peanut.

'The thing is, the RAZERs are on to us. As I said, they are tracking every resident of Chroma. You and your friends have a huge advantage. They don't know about you. And they certainly don't know about all of that,' said Mrs M, glancing at the art materials in Peanut's bandolier. 'With that creative firepower, we'd have a fighting chance.'

She leaned forwards on her elbows. 'But first, why don't you tell me exactly how you got here?'

29
The Key

Peanut turned to Rockwell. He shook his head slightly. She swallowed, deciding to trust Mrs M with their secret.

'Well. I, er, drew a door in my bedroom.'

'You *drew* a door in your bedroom?'

'Yes, and then I opened it and walked through. And then we were here. In Chroma. By the signposts.'

'Really? That's *very* interesting.' Mrs M nodded. 'And what, may I ask, did you draw the door with?'

'This.' Peanut pulled the pencil from its slot on her bandolier. Mrs M's eyes widened.

'Where did you get this, Peanut?'

'I, er, I found it.'

'You found it? Forgive me, but I'm not sure I believe you,' said Mrs M. Her eyes hadn't left the pencil. 'Remarkable. Truly remarkable. With this, we might just be able to . . .'

'To what?' asked Rockwell. 'What are you talking about?'

'I'm sorry. I'm forgetting myself.' She stood up.

'You, Peanut, you have something that Mr White would give his eye teeth for. Something for which he'd trade every single item that he has confiscated from the people of

Chroma.' Her voice became little more than a whisper. 'Unless I'm very much mistaken, that little yellow pencil that you have there is "Little Tail". Otherwise known as "Pencil Number One". It's Conté's prototype.'

Peanut looked down at the yellow pencil.

'Your pencil is a key. *The* key. To unlimited travel between Chroma and your world. Whenever you like, you can just draw a door and walk between the worlds. It is extremely powerful.'

'Can I use it to help rescue Mr M?'

'You can use it to help rescue all of us, Peanut. That and all of those other "weapons" you have strapped to your chest: the paint, the spray, the markers.'

Peanut thought for a minute. Then she stood up and rummaged around in the front pocket of her dungarees.

'Can I ask you a question, Mrs M?'

'Of course you can, my dear.'

'Have you ever seen this man?' She showed Mrs M the strip of passport photos of her and her dad.

Mrs M removed her glasses and had a good look.

'Ah yes. Of course I remember him. Young Gary was one of the first. A true Resistance hero and a very brave chap, as I recall. He was carrying out a lot of important work for us until—'

'You know him?!' gasped Peanut. 'You've seen him?'

Mrs M looked at Peanut and then back at the photograph in her hand. 'Ah yes, I can see the resemblance. Your father,

I presume? The apple didn't fall too far from the tree, did it?'

'Yes. Yes, he's my dad! Do you know where he is now?' She was barely able to contain her excitement.

'Well, I've not seen him for a very long time, I'm afraid. He was here, though, carrying out a top-secret spying mission for us. And he was doing a brilliant job, bringing us a lot of highly valuable information at great personal risk. But then, one day, he just . . . didn't come back.'

'About a year ago?' said Peanut. 'Er, I guess that would be about twenty-four years in your time?'

'Sounds about right,' said Mrs M sadly. 'We did our best to find out what had happened but there has been no intelligence since he disappeared.'

'Do you think Mr White has got him? Do you think he has been locked up in the Spire too?'

'I can't say for certain, but that would be my guess.' She stood up, walked across the room and rested Peanut's photographs against the picture of her husband. 'Maybe they're together, keeping each other's spirits up . . . ?'

'Don't worry, Mrs M, we'll find them!' insisted Little-Bit.

'Hang on, LB. What do you mean, "we"? I said you could stay until we found Doodle's owners, and then you would have to go home,' said Peanut.

'I'm coming with you,' said Little-Bit firmly. 'He's my daddy too!'

'No way!' said Rockwell.

'Why not? So you can have Peanut all to yourself?'

'No! Because, er, because . . . just *because*, all right?'

'Peanut,' said Little-Bit with a sly grin. 'Wouldn't it be awful if Mummy found out about what you were up to. Especially as you're already in such big trouble cos of all the detentions and everything.'

Peanut sighed reluctantly. 'OK, LB, but you have to do exactly what Rockwell and I tell you. At all times.'

'Er, who said anything about *me* coming?' said Rockwell incredulously. 'Peanut, you can't be serious. We can't possibly do this! What about school?'

'What *about* school?' Peanut snapped. 'There are some things in life that are far more important than school! The fact that the world's entire supply of creative energy is at risk of being destroyed, for example. And what about this poor lady's husband? And my dad? I haven't seen him for an entire year! If there's any possibility that he is being held against his will here in Chroma I have to at least *try* to rescue him. Surely you can understand that!'

'B-b-but what about my differentiation homework? And the physics test?'

'Remember what I told you about the weird thing that happens with time in Chroma?' said Peanut. 'Last time I was here, I spent over three hours playing with Doodle, but when

I got home I'd only been gone for about ten minutes.'

'Your friend is right,' said Mrs M. 'Time is linear, but it can move at different speeds. The chances are, you would still make it to school on time.'

'Besides,' Peanut looked at Rockwell, 'I thought we were friends.'

Rockwell couldn't stop the smile from appearing on his face.

'Study buddies, actually.' He sighed. 'OK. I'll do it. But only if you promise to test me on my differentiation on the way to school when we get back.'

'Deal.'

Peanut tightened her grip on the pencil. 'OK, so how do we get to the Spire?'

30
Peanut's Mission

The next hour was spent studying the map with Mrs M as she worked out a route through the city.

'We need you to stay out of sight for as long as possible,' she said, 'so, in the first instance, I'm going to send you through the Ink District via the Black Mountains. Once you've crossed Inky Lake you can access the Spire via the Strip. It will be easier to keep a low profile when there are more people around. You can blend in.'

'How will we know that we're going the right way?' asked Peanut.

'Well, you'll have the map, for starters. And Doodle will be with you. He knows the city well and the RAZERs won't pay any attention to a dog. He can be your guide.'

Doodle wagged his tail and barked his approval.

'We also have a number of Resistance agents that I will contact and brief with regard to your mission. I'll arrange for them to meet you at key points on your journey to help you on your way. I'm afraid I can't give you any more details about these agents at the moment for security reasons. Their anonymity is key to their safety. Know this though: you will have a lot of people rooting for you, Peanut, even if you're not always aware of it.'

Mrs M pulled the blue pencil from her hair and drew a dotted line on the map. 'This is the path you should follow. I will make sure someone is there to meet you on the north bank of Inky Lake to advise you of your next move. You must get

there before nightfall.' She handed Peanut the map and a small, hand-painted compass. 'The good people of Chroma will thank you for doing this, Peanut. If you do manage to rescue Mr M, our chances of defeating White will be vastly improved. My husband is a brilliant man.'

'My dad is brilliant too,' said Peanut. 'He'll be happy to help as well, I just know it. We promise that we'll do our best to bring both of them back with us.'

'I know you will,' said the old lady.

Mrs M disappeared through the triangular door and put together a small hamper with enough food to last them for a couple of days. When she returned, she led the gang up the stairs towards the hatch.

'Now, promise me you'll look after our new friends, Doodle. I want everyone back in one piece.'

'Don't worry about us, Mrs M,' said Peanut. 'We'll be back with your husband before you know it.'

'And our daddy!' shouted Little-Bit.

They waved goodbye, and the four intrepid adventurers set off on their mission.

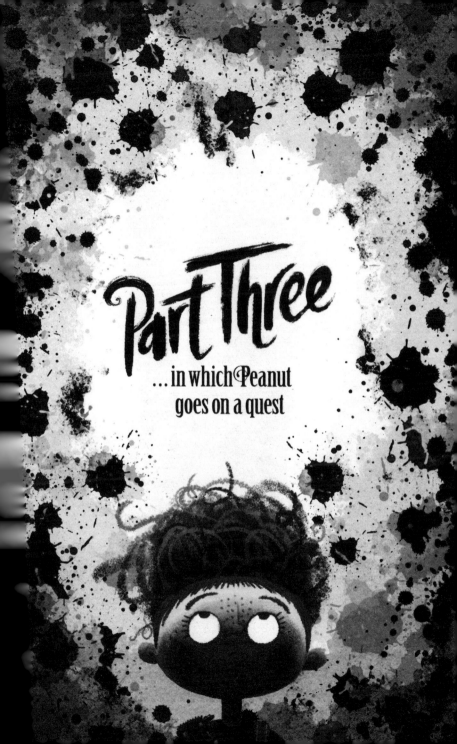

Part Three

...in which Peanut
goes on a quest

31
Cages

oodle led the three children east across the deserted plains of the North Draw towards the Ink District. In the distance, they could see mountains rising from the snow, painted black against the pale sky. As per Mrs M's dotted blue line, the group stuck close to the city limits and headed for the forested area known as Sketchwood.

'I've been thinking,' said Rockwell as they walked. 'What happens if you lose that pencil? We would have absolutely no way of getting back home again, would we?'

'Didn't Mrs M say something about a portal?' replied Peanut.

'No. She said there were rumours of a portal, but that no actual evidence of one has ever been found.'

'Oh well, in that case, I guess we'd be stuck here until we

found another way home,' said Peanut, trying to sound cheerful. 'After all, Dad must have got here by other means. He can't have used Little Tail cos it was hidden in the box in my room.'

'Well, I don't want to be stuck here, thank you very much.' Rockwell scratched the back of his head. 'If I'm late handing in my differentiation homework I'll be in *such* trouble.'

'Do you always follow the rules?' Peanut asked as they trooped along as quickly as they could.

'Well, yes. If I didn't, I'd lose my scholarship and they'd kick me out. Immediately. No second chances. Absolutely none! You know St Hubert's.'

'I do.' Peanut gave him a quick, sympathetic smile. 'In that case I'd better make sure I don't lose the pencil. We can't have you getting in trouble, can we?'

Peanut was keen to reach the shelter of the trees as soon as possible, given what she'd heard about Mr White and his RAZERs. If he discovered they were in Chroma, they would definitely be in a fix.

After more slow trudging, they finally reached the edge of the woods.

'We made it,' whispered Rockwell. 'Which way now, Doodle?'

The dog wagged his tail and started winding his way through the black tree trunks. The children followed.

All of a sudden, Doodle stopped walking and cocked his

head to one side. Up ahead was a small clearing, in the middle of which stood a solitary, slim figure holding a walking stick. He was looking straight up into the canopy of a particularly tall tree. Instinctively, Peanut crouched down and put her hand over Little-Bit's mouth. She knew that her little sister would find calling out hard to resist.

'What do we do?' she whispered to Rockwell.

'I don't know. He doesn't look like a robot, but maybe they're masters of disguise.'

Doodle sniffed noisily at the ground. After a few seconds his tail started to wag and he trotted out into the clearing.

'Hello, little fella,' said the man. 'What are you doing all the way out here on your own?'

Doodle allowed him to stroke his back, before turning to face the children.

'Woof! Woof!'

'I think he's saying that it's OK,' said Peanut as she removed her hand from Little-Bit's mouth.

'Hello there!' shouted the little girl immediately, before running out into the clearing.

The man looked startled as Peanut, Rockwell and Little-Bit emerged from the trees.

'Well, bless my soul. Children!' He looked down at Peanut's bandolier. 'And children carrying . . . contraband. Just about the last thing

I expected to find on my little walk. I'm guessing that you're not from these parts.'

'No. We're not,' said Peanut.

'Well, if I were you I wouldn't risk being out in the open carrying pencils and pens like that. Ooh, are those watercolours? I haven't seen a set of watercolours for such a long time.' He looked wistful.

'Excuse me for asking,' said Little-Bit, 'but what were you looking at just now? In the tree?'

The man glanced upwards. 'I was looking at those.'

The children followed his gaze and saw, hanging in the branches, three ornate black cages. Inside each one was a large bird, about the size of a peacock. They had crests on their heads – one red, one gold and one green – and the most beautiful, multicoloured tail feathers, at least a metre long.

'What are *they*?' gasped Little-Bit.

'Kaleidoscoppi,' said the man. 'Just captured, I'd wager. Tragic.'

'Captured? Who would want to trap such beautiful animals?'

'Do I really need to tell you?' The man sighed.

Peanut shook her head.

'The kaleidoscoppi have been flying free in Chroma for centuries. It is said that their song has the power to inspire amazing ideas in whoever hears it.' He bent down to stroke Doodle. 'They were always few and far between, but since Mr White took control they are hardly ever spotted. I guess this is why.'

Right on cue, a beautiful tune came from inside one of the cages. It sounded like two flutes playing in perfect harmony.

Suddenly, Peanut had a thought. She looked at the tree trunk and turned to Rockwell.

'Do you think you could support me on your shoulders so that I could reach that branch?'

'Er, yes. I think I probably could.'

'OK. Give me a leg up, then.'

Rockwell leaned against the trunk as Peanut clambered up on to his shoulders. She just about managed to grab the branch that the cages were hanging from and haul herself up on to it. She then shimmied along it until she was directly above the three captured birds. Carefully, she removed Little Tail from its slot on her bandolier, reached down to the first cage and started working away at it with the rubber on the end of the pencil. To everybody's surprise, the bars started to disappear, and within seconds there was a hole in the first cage big enough for the red-topped kaleidoscoppi to fit through. With a single flap of his wings, he flew up and out of the opening. Two minutes later, all three birds were tracing circles in the sky, high above the trees.

'You did it!' shouted the man. 'You set them free!'

A loud fluttering sound and a sudden rush of air filled the clearing as the gold-topped bird swooped back down and hovered in front of Peanut. His face just inches from hers, he looked into her eyes, trilled several bars of his hypnotic melody and nodded before shooting back to join his friends.

'I think he said "thank you".' The man smiled.

32
An Ink Storm

After saying goodbye to the stranger, Peanut, Rockwell, Little-Bit and Doodle carried on winding their way through Sketchwood. As they walked, the path got gradually steeper and the scattering of trees became more dense.

'My ears are popping,' said Little-Bit. 'It's just like that time we went on holiday to Menorca and I had to have seventeen sherbet lemons on the plane just to keep my eardrums from exploding.'

'I think we've crossed the border into the Ink District,' said Rockwell, noticing the difference in the trees. 'I'm guessing that we're in the foothills of the Black Mountains.'

'Peanut, have you got any sherbet lemons?' Little-Bit had

both hands clamped on to the sides of her head.

Peanut pulled out the pencil and air-drew a boiled sweet. She plucked it from in front of her and handed it to her sister.

'Try this,' she said.

Little-Bit took it and put it in her mouth. 'YUCK! It tastes of tuna!'

Within half an hour the incline had increased to such an extent that the group found themselves using their hands almost as much as their feet. After pulling themselves up and over a fallen tree on a particularly steep section of slope, they sat down to catch their breath.

Peanut looked at the sky. 'It's getting dark. What time is it?'

'Only about two thirty,' said Rockwell. 'Hang on. Did you feel that?'

'Feel what?'

'That. Something wet. There it is again!'

Doodle ran over to the biggest tree on the slope and sat underneath its branches.

'What's that on your face?' said Peanut to Rockwell. 'Running down your forehead?'

The boy wiped it and looked at his hand.

Splat! Splat! Two black drops of liquid landed on his palm. And then . . . the heavens opened.

Hundreds of fat orbs of oily liquid tumbled from the sky, exploding on the ground leaving a dark splatter pattern like a Jackson Pollock painting.

'QUICK!' shouted Rockwell. 'Get under the tree with Doodle. It's raining ink!'

The three of them, soaked and streaked with black liquid, scrambled over to where Doodle was sheltering.

'You look like you got into a paint fight in the art room,' laughed Rockwell, looking over at Peanut.

'Ha! Don't pretend you've ever been in an art room,' she replied, smiling.

'Guys. Mummy always says that you shouldn't shelter underneath trees in a storm,' declared Little-Bit. 'She says that it's much better to be a bit wet than it is to be a bit electrocuted by lightning.'

'Oh, come on,' chuckled Rockwell. 'That's *such* a myth! Did you know that the odds of a human being struck by lightning are approximately ten million to one? In fact, you're considerably more likely to be crushed by an intergalactic meteor or eaten by a hippo—'

CRACK!

The explosion was so loud that it left the children's ears ringing. Peanut could smell burning. She looked up and saw bright orange flames licking the top of the tree.

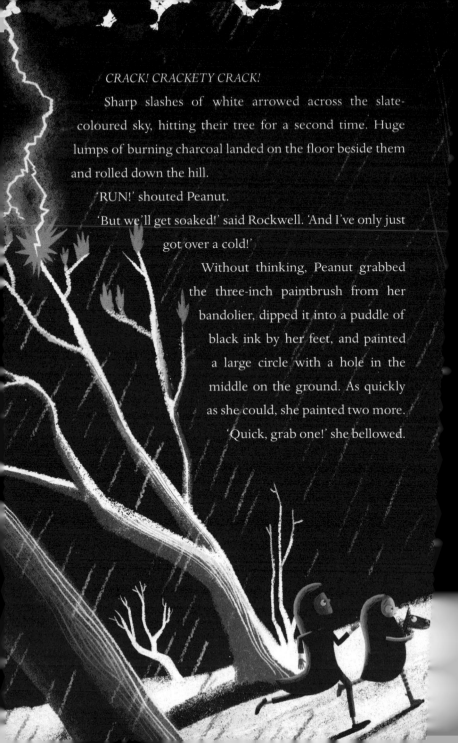

CRACK! CRACKETY CRACK!

Sharp slashes of white arrowed across the slate-coloured sky, hitting their tree for a second time. Huge lumps of burning charcoal landed on the floor beside them and rolled down the hill.

'RUN!' shouted Peanut.

'But we'll get soaked!' said Rockwell. 'And I've only just got over a cold!'

Without thinking, Peanut grabbed the three-inch paintbrush from her bandolier, dipped it into a puddle of black ink by her feet, and painted a large circle with a hole in the middle on the ground. As quickly as she could, she painted two more.

'Quick, grab one!' she bellowed.

'Let's hope the paintbrush works just like Little Tail!'

The three children each grabbed a painted disc and threw it over their heads, poking their faces through the holes.

'It worked!' shouted Little-Bit.

Peanut scooped up Doodle, pulled him under her new poncho, and the four of them ran out into the pouring black rain, away from the burning tree.

33
The Flying Fish

The thick, black droplets continued to fall as the intrepid foursome made their way up the mountain. The ground was slick with mud, so they were wearing hand-drawn crampons on their feet for a bit of extra grip.

Peanut was tired. Not only was she carrying the dog but she had also filled the four empty water bottles on her back with inky rainwater. She was starting to doubt her sense of direction, especially since a mist had descended.

After a couple of hours, the rain slowed and the tiny cracks of daylight started to get bigger until, eventually, they expanded to reveal a huge sky. At last they had reached the top of the mountain.

They sat on the snowy ground and took off their ponchos. Doodle jumped from Peanut's arms and stretched, while Rockwell opened his rucksack, pulled out the small hamper that Mrs M had given them and handed out sandwiches.

'Just look at that view,' he said between mouthfuls of ham and tomato.

They were above the cloudline. Beneath them, a grey, fluffy sea stretched into the distance, occasionally interrupted by other mountain tops that broke the surface like shark fins in the Pacific Ocean.

'Awesome,' whispered Little-Bit.

Peanut took the map from her bandolier and unfolded it. 'So, by my reckoning, we are here.' She pulled out the compass. 'We need to start heading south-east, down towards Inky Lake.'

Doodle barked his approval.

Then something very strange happened. A small object, no bigger than a tennis ball, shot up through the clouds and hovered in the air ten metres in front of them.

'What is *that*?' gasped Rockwell

'It looks like . . . a *fish*?' spluttered Peanut.

'A fish?' Little-Bit stood up. 'But how could a fish fly this high?'

'How could a fish fly *at all*?' said Rockwell. All four were on their feet now, and Doodle was barking loudly.

Its shiny body was round and covered in spikes, with a large, brassy tail fanning out behind it. Its eyes, glowing green, were looking straight at the children. With a click and a whirr, they suddenly widened and changed from green to red. A small door slid open where its mouth should be and a deafening, high-pitched sound filled the air. It then shot back down into the cloud and disappeared.

'Something's telling me that what just happened wasn't a good thing,' said Rockwell.

'I agree,' said Peanut. 'I think we need to get out of here.'

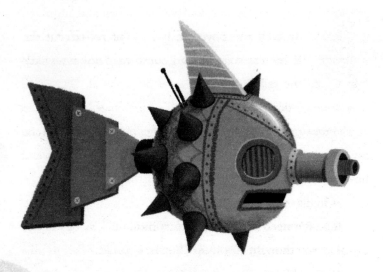

34
A Bobsleigh Ride

Rockwell had never been a fan of roller coasters. If he was completely honest, he'd not even liked the tall slide at the local playground. He would only ever go down it sitting on his mum's lap which, when you're ten, could be a bit embarrassing. That's why, when he saw what Peanut was drawing with her magic pencil, several beads of sweat appeared on his brow.

'Is that . . . a bobsleigh?' he asked.

'Yes. We need to get down this mountain as quickly as possible, so I thought this would be our best bet.'

'Right.' He swallowed. 'And you know how to drive a bobsleigh, do you?'

'Nope. Don't have a clue.'

'Right.' He swallowed again.

Peanut started drawing what looked like a long, narrow bathtub on skis with a steering wheel at one end. As she rushed to colour in her outlined drawing with a wash of black rain ink, the faint alarm call of the levitating mechanical fish rang out in the distance. Even Rockwell had to admit that a fast escape was a good idea. But that didn't mean he was happy about it.

'Finished!' Peanut put her art equipment back in the bandolier. 'Right, I'll drive. Doodle can sit by my feet and LB, you sit behind me. Rockwell, you're in the back. OK. Everybody in.'

They took their places. Rockwell started to feel a bit sick.

'Actually, Rockwell. Thinking

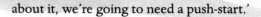

about it, we're going to need a push-start.'

'You want *me* to do it?'

'Yes. I've got to steer. Come on, get out and give us a push. Hurry up, that thing looked like it meant business and I'm guessing whoever it's calling will be here soon!'

Rockwell clambered out of the sleigh and walked around to the back. It was pointing straight towards a very steep downward slope that ran for about thirty metres before

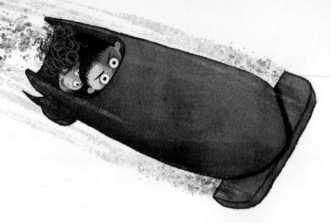

disappearing into the clouds below them. He shook his head. 'I could be practising my differentiation now,' he said out loud. 'But instead I'm—'

'GO!' shouted Peanut.

He was surprised at how light the sleigh felt. It didn't need much of a shove to get going, and when it did, it gained momentum rapidly. He just about managed to haul himself back inside before it tipped forwards and plunged down into the clouds.

The children were forced backwards as they hurtled down the mountain. Peanut squinted against the onrushing wind, steering left and then right and then left again, narrowly avoiding tree after tree.

Rockwell, meanwhile, had his head between his knees and was praying for a quick death. He realised, to his relief, that the sound of the fish's alarm had faded away. It had, however, been replaced by a deafening, high-pitched whooping sound. He glanced up to see Little-Bit with both her hands in the air and her head tipped back.

'THIIIIIISSSS IIIIIIIISSSS AAAAWWWESOOOOMME!' she hollered.

Rockwell put his head back down, just as they took a chicane at full speed. *Bang*. His left shoulder slammed into the side of the sleigh. *Whack*. Right shoulder. *Bang*. Left again.

'THIS IS REALLY HURTING!' he shouted. 'CAN WE STOP NOW PLEASE?'

'ER, ABOUT THAT . . .' replied Peanut. 'I FORGOT TO DRAW ANY BRAKES.'

Rockwell shut his eyes tightly and cursed the fact that he wasn't going to get to fulfil his potential as one of the nation's greatest ever engineers. He was at least thankful that he had managed to finally understand the laws of thermodynamics during last night's revision session.

'RIGHT! HOLD TIGHT EVERYBODY!' bellowed Peanut. 'I'M GOING TO TRY SOMETHING . . .'

All four passengers were suddenly thrown violently to the left and Rockwell felt the entire sleigh start to tip. They travelled for a full ten seconds leaning at a seemingly impossible angle before eventually levelling out and, miracle of miracles, starting to slow down. Rockwell didn't lift his head from between his knees until he was absolutely certain that they had come to a complete standstill.

He groaned. 'I think I'm going to be sick.'

35
The Bridge

Rockwell looked up. The clouds were a long way above them now and, although it was still raining, it was more drizzle than stair rods. Little-Bit leaped from the bobsleigh.

'That,' she shouted, 'was the best ride I've ever been on! I can't believe you managed to surf around that snow bowl, Peanut. A genius move! It was *totally* radical!'

'*I* can't believe I forgot the brakes.' Peanut was furious

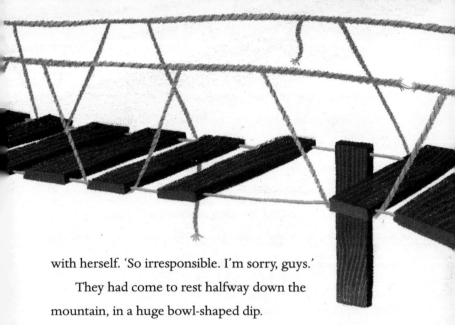

with herself. 'So irresponsible. I'm sorry, guys.'

They had come to rest halfway down the mountain, in a huge bowl-shaped dip.

'So now what?' Rockwell said.

'Well, I reckon we've put a fair distance between ourselves and the screaming fish,' replied Peanut, 'but, even so, we'd better get a shift on.' She looked towards the edge of the bowl. 'Wait. Is that a bridge?'

Sure enough, there was a narrow and very rickety-looking rope bridge stretching out over a gorge. It sloped down, at a slightly terrifying angle, to a ridge thirty metres below them on the other side. A further thirty metres beneath that was a huge expanse of dark water that looked like it had been painted with very thin poster paints.

'That must be Inky Lake,' said Peanut. 'Come on. There's no time to waste.'

They walked to the edge of the bowl where the bridge was anchored. Peanut noticed that several of the painted planks of wood that made up the decking were either rotting away or missing entirely, and at least one of the pencil ropes that the bridge was suspended from looked very straggly and worn.

Peanut took a deep breath. 'OK, I'll go first. Doodle and Little-Bit can follow, and Rockwell, you bring up the rear.'

Gingerly she put her right foot on the first plank. It moved much more than she thought it would, dropping several inches as she put the tiniest bit of weight on it. She grasped the waist-height ropes that acted as both handrails and main source of suspension, and held tight. She carefully took another step. Again, the bridge moved more than she would have liked, but this time sideways. She felt like she was standing on a hammock.

'It-it's fine. We've just got to take it slowly.'

Five terrifying, wobbly steps later she realised that the others hadn't moved an inch. Doodle was now lying on his belly and looking like he wasn't going anywhere.

'Well? What are you waiting for?' she shouted.

At that exact moment, a loud, snapping sound came

from somewhere in the middle of the gorge and one of the handrail ropes instantly lost all of its tension. It came flying back towards the group like a jet-propelled snake. The entire stretch of decking rotated ninety degrees and disappeared from under Peanut's feet. She grabbed the one remaining handrail.

Little-Bit screamed.

'I'm OK, I'm OK!' shouted Peanut unconvincingly as her feet dangled over the void beneath her. 'Quick! Pull me back up!'

Then there was a second snap.

36
The Fall

Everything was moving in slow motion.

The rope she was holding turned to jelly.

She was moving forward. Rolling.

Cliff face.

She was upside down.

Her right hand was free.

Sky.

She was upright again.

Cliff face.

Where did everybody go?

Rocks.

Sky.

Cliff face.

Rocks.

Sky.

The clouds were moving away from her.

Cliff face.

She looked down.

Rocks.

The wind was pounding her face.

Sky.

She reached with her right hand.

Cliff face.

She grabbed something and pulled.

Rocks.

She held it above her head.

Sky.

She pressed the button.

3·7
The Lifeline

'PEEANUUUTT?'

Little-Bit's voice sounded as if it were coming from a long way above her.

'PEEEAAANNNNUUUTTTT? ARE YOU OK?'

'I THINK SO.' She was clinging on to something above her head and swaying slightly over the ravine.

'OK. NOW HOLD ON TIGHT.' It was Rockwell this time. 'WE'RE GOING TO PULL YOU UP.'

A few seconds later she started moving upwards. Her arm muscles were burning. She looked up to see that she was holding on to the can of spray paint from her bandolier which, in turn, was connected to the very top of the cliff face by a long, rubbery

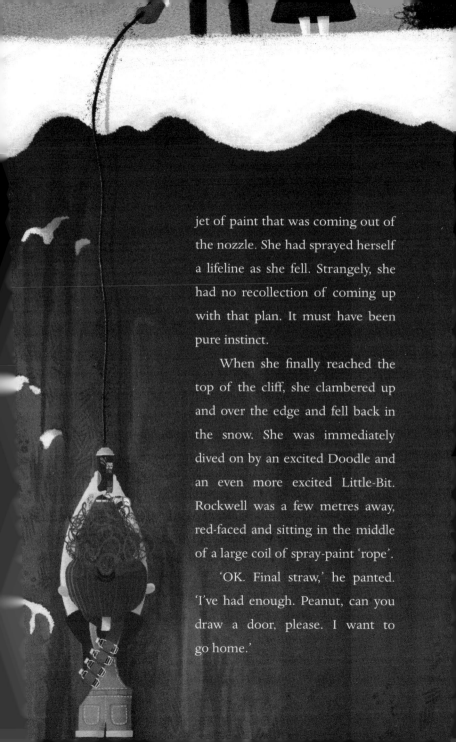

jet of paint that was coming out of the nozzle. She had sprayed herself a lifeline as she fell. Strangely, she had no recollection of coming up with that plan. It must have been pure instinct.

When she finally reached the top of the cliff, she clambered up and over the edge and fell back in the snow. She was immediately dived on by an excited Doodle and an even more excited Little-Bit. Rockwell was a few metres away, red-faced and sitting in the middle of a large coil of spray-paint 'rope'.

'OK. Final straw,' he panted. 'I've had enough. Peanut, can you draw a door, please. I want to go home.'

38
Rockwell's Brilliant Idea

Peanut and Little-Bit stood at the edge of the ravine looking down at the remains of the bridge hanging next to the cliff face.

'So what do we do now?' asked Little-Bit.

'I'm not sure, LB. All I know is that Mrs M said that we've got to be at the lake before it gets dark.'

'So, about that door . . .' said Rockwell from behind them. He was still sitting in the snow.

'Have either of you got any bright ideas as to how we can get down to the lake?' asked Peanut, peering over the edge.

'Well, you could always just jump off the cliff,' suggested Little-Bit cheerily.

'Very funny.'

'Actually . . . that might just work,' said Rockwell. There was a look of intense concentration on his face.

Peanut frowned. 'Well, there's no doubt that we'd get there quickly if we did that. It's just that we would be a bit too, y'know, dead.'

'Not necessarily.' Rockwell stood up, strolled towards the sisters and looked over the edge. Then he licked his finger and looked up into the sky. He nodded. 'Interesting.'

'What are you doing?' asked Peanut.

'I'm coming up with a brilliant idea,' he said drily. 'You *could* jump off of the cliff if you had the right equipment.'

'What . . . equipment? A parachute?' said Little-Bit.

'There's not enough height for a parachute. Some sort of simple wing design would work, though. With something to hold on to suspended underneath it.'

'I don't understand,' said Peanut.

'Funnily enough, I was reading about thermodynamics last night and, apparently, if you are high up on a cliff edge, for example, holding an aerofoil, or a wing, above your head, and you run at about fifteen miles per hour, you'll get enough air moving over the upper surface of the wing to make the pressure above it drop considerably. This will generate the lift that will enable you to . . . take off.'

'You mean that you would *fly*?'

'Well, you would glide, certainly. Once you were over the

edge of the cliff and in the air, gravity would slowly pull you back to earth, but at the same time you would be propelled forward.' He looked down at the lake. 'In theory, you should be able to jump off the edge and steer yourself down.'

Peanut handed Rockwell the pencil. 'Sounds brilliant. Show me what this wing looks like.'

'But, I can't draw! I'm rubbish at art!'

'Nonsense. Just imagine that you're drawing a diagram in your physics exercise book and that you're really trying to impress old Death Breath.'

Rockwell started drawing a shape in front of him. The line, as always, seemed to flow from the tip and hang, suspended in the air.

'Whoa! This is so cool,' he said.

Peanut smiled.

A few minutes later, Rockwell's diagram was finished.

'There. What do you think?'

'Not bad, for someone who can't draw. Not bad at all,' said Peanut. 'This one will be just perfect for me and Little-Bit. Now you need to draw another one for you and Doodle.'

'Me and Doodle? No way. I told you, I still want to go home.'

'Oh, come on, Rockwell, we need you. I can't carry Doodle as well as LB. And anyway, don't you want to find out if your brilliant idea works?'

'Yeah, come on, Rockwell. Don't be such a *baby*,' said Little-Bit. Doodle wound himself in a figure of eight around Rockwell's legs.

Rockwell shook his head. He knew when he was beaten. 'Well, I guess I could stay a *little* longer. It would be kind of cool to test out my idea in a real-world environment. But just so you know, I still want to go home as soon as I can. OK?'

'Whatever,' said Peanut happily. 'You draw, I'll get colouring.'

39
Flying

Peanut and Rockwell stood six metres apart facing down the slope. Little-Bit was strapped to her sister's back in a hastily painted harness and Doodle was facing forwards in a similarly sketchy papoose on Rockwell's chest. The classmates were holding on to the bottom side of a marker-pen triangle, the top point of which was connected to a large, flat, arrowhead-shaped wing. Several other thin pencil lines ran, seemingly randomly, between the

passengers and various points on the wing. Rockwell had told Peanut that they were very important 'for stability'.

Peanut looked across. 'You ready?'

'Not really,' stammered Rockwell. He felt exactly the same way as he did the time his dad made him jump off the middle diving board at the swimming pool. 'Just trust in the physics.'

'Yes, all right, Einstein. Let's just get it over with, shall we?' Peanut was feeling more nervous than she wanted to admit.

'OK. Here we go. After three, we run as fast as we can towards the edge of the cliff and we jump off.'

Peanut took a deep breath.

'ONE . . . TWO . . . THREE!'

Neither of them moved.

'Peanut, I don't think I can do it. My legs don't seem to be working.'

'Mine are a bit shaky too.' She felt a shudder of fear that seemed to belong to someone else.

Suddenly they heard a noise from further up the slope. They turned to see several silvery objects moving very quickly towards them across the snow, all of them emitting a familiar, high-pitched sound.

'Are they . . . men?' shouted Rockwell.

'Whatever they are,' replied Peanut, 'I think it's time we left. LET'S GO!'

The two children ran as fast as they could down the hill. The huge wings felt as light as a feather one second and then as heavy as a rock the next, but the steepness of the slope was in their favour. As they approached the edge of the cliff, every

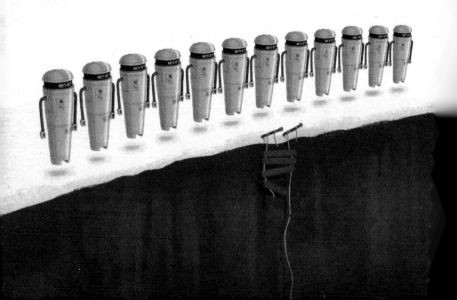

instinct Rockwell had was telling him to throw himself to the ground, but somehow he kept going. By the time they reached the edge, they were travelling at such a speed that he couldn't have stopped even if he had wanted to.

And then . . . the ground disappeared from beneath their feet. They didn't drop an inch. They just kept on moving forwards, legs still pumping furiously in the air.

'WE'RE FLYING!' Peanut laughed.

'IT WORKED!' shouted Rockwell.

As they sailed over the abyss, everything suddenly felt very calm. The world opened up below them and the only sound was the quiet rush of the wind as it moved across the wings.

Little-Bit looked behind them. Twelve tall, silver robots come to a stop on the clifftop above the broken bridge. They appeared to be floating about thirty centimetres above the ground and their eyes were glowing bright red.

'Peanut, I think those things chasing us might be . . .'

'RAZERs . . .' said Peanut. 'I think they know we're here.'

40
Ka-Boom!

As they drifted through the air, Peanut and Rockwell found that they could steer their gliders by shifting their weight from side to side.

'This is FUN!' shouted Rockwell as he carved a long, curving arc through the sky.

'Look down there!' shouted Peanut.

Far below them to the left, they could see a small town at the foot of the mountain range. It mainly consisted of low-rise buildings in a grid formation, but every now and then a sharp, black shard shot upwards at a dramatic angle.

'I bet that's Manga Town,' said Little-Bit. 'I noticed it on the map earlier. I really want to go there.'

From this height, it was easier to appreciate the scale of

everything. The lake was huge. It wasn't particularly wide, but it stretched for miles lengthways in both directions. A feeling of despair washed over Peanut as she wondered how on earth they would find Mrs M's Resistance contact, given that she had told them so little about who or what to look out for. The words 'needle' and 'haystack' came to mind. Despair was soon replaced by steadfast resolve, however, when she pictured her dad locked up in the Spire. No matter how hard this mission was, she was determined to succeed. For him.

'At least there's no snow down here!' shouted Rockwell, wrenching Peanut from her daydream. 'Where shall we aim to land?'

As Peanut searched for a suitable landing spot among the trees bordering the lake, something silver caught her eye.

'Did you see that?' she shouted.

She needn't have asked.

Flying either side of Rockwell, about a metre away, were two mechanical fish, exactly like the one they had encountered at the top of the mountain. Their telescopic eyes glowed red and were firmly trained on the boy as he flew.

'Peanut! What do I do?'

In a panic, she had several thoughts at the same time. Was there any way she could take them out right now? What should she do when the fish sounded their alarms? How could

they escape the RAZERs that would probably be waiting for them when they landed?

What happened next, however, came as a total surprise. The fishes' eyes suddenly switched from red to white and they both stopped dead in their tracks. The two gliders travelled another few metres and then . . . KA-BOOM! The fish exploded behind them.

'W-w-what just happened?' shrieked Rockwell.

'I have no idea.' Peanut shifted her weight forward so that her glider started to descend more sharply. 'But I think we need to land and find cover as quickly as possible.'

41
Looking for the Resistance

In hindsight, maybe it was a mistake to let Little-Bit loose with the pencil and the watercolours. Peanut had eventually given in to her sister's pleas to let her draw a simple tent for them to shelter in, mainly because (a) since they had landed, Peanut had been busy rubbing out the hang-gliders, thus removing any evidence of their arrival at the lake, and (b) Rockwell and Doodle were searching the area for Mrs M's Resistance contact.

'I mean, it's very nice,' said Peanut, looking at the tent, 'but are you sure it won't attract any unwanted attention?'

Before Little-Bit could answer, Rockwell appeared from behind one of the ink trees with Doodle snuffling at his heel.

'Er, what is *that*?' he said, pointing to the tent.

'Don't worry. We're deep in the forest. No one will be able to see it.'

'Are you kidding? I reckon it's probably visible from space!'

Peanut handed him a freshly drawn cup of tea. 'Did you guys have any luck?'

'Nope.' He took a sip and winced. It tasted of gravy. 'Look, it's almost dark, and I don't know about you, but I'm exhausted. Plus, the fact that we are currently being hunted by a massive army of evil silver floating robots is making me feel a tad nervous. Maybe we should start looking again in the morning when my courage levels have had a chance to replenish.'

Peanut couldn't stifle a yawn. She nodded.

'And then when we find them,' continued Rockwell, 'you can draw me that door.'

'Oh, you're not still banging on about the door, are you?' said Little-Bit from inside the tent. 'I was just beginning to like you.'

'Shut it, pipsqueak,' grunted Rockwell. 'Isn't it dinner time?'

After they'd polished off the last of Mrs M's sandwiches, Peanut drew three simple sleeping bags, some very fluffy-looking pillows (painted with the thickest brush) and a cosy, fleece-lined bed for Doodle. She put them into Little-Bit's tent and the four of them settled down for the night.

'Do you think Mummy will be worried about us?' asked Little-Bit, snuggling into her warm bed.

'No. She'll probably only just be getting to work.' whispered Peanut. 'Remember time moves at a different rate here in Chroma. Are you missing her? Would you like me to tell you a story?'

There was no reply, just the gentle sound of Little-Bit, Rockwell and Doodle's breathing.

Peanut yawned again. Just as her eyes were starting to close, she heard a faint rustling noise outside the tent. At first she thought she'd imagined it, but then there it was again. A twig snapped. She sat up, holding her breath. There was definitely someone, or something, out there.

She grabbed Little Tail, summoned all of her courage and burst out through the tent flap. And there, in the moonlight, was . . . THE BIGGEST, MOST FEROCIOUS-LOOKING ALLIGATOR SHE HAD EVER SEEN IN HER ENTIRE LIFE!

42

Jonathan Higginbottom

Peanut tried to scream, but the only sound that came out was a rather pathetic whimper. It was, however, enough to wake Little-Bit, Rockwell and Doodle, whose heads instantly appeared through the tent flap.

'OH. MY. GOD!' yelled Rockwell.

'AAAALLLLLLIIIIGGGGAAAAAATTTTOOORRRRR!' shouted Little-Bit.

Doodle disappeared back inside the tent.

'Oh come now, didn't your parents ever tell you not to judge a book by its cover?'

Little-Bit stopped screaming.

Peanut dropped the pencil.

Unless they were very much mistaken, the terrifying-looking creature in front of them had just . . . spoken. Not only that, but he had the friendliest, softest voice imaginable. He sounded, well, nice.

'I can assure you that there is nothing to be scared of,' continued the alligator. 'I am aware that I might initially appear a bit . . . threatening, and, Lord knows, I wish that wasn't the case, but once you get to know me, you'll see that, despite these looks, I'm a big softie.'

Rockwell scratched his head. Little-Bit's mouth was hanging open.

The alligator smiled, revealing

at least a hundred razor-sharp teeth. 'Allow me to introduce myself. My name is Jonathan Higginbottom. I gather you are in need of some assistance.'

'You?' gasped Peanut. 'You're Mrs M's Resistance contact?'

'Correct.' Jonathan Higginbottom grinned.

'But . . . but . . . you're a . . . massive alligator,' said Little-Bit.

'Ten out of ten for observation.'

'But how does an alligator get to join the Resistance?'

'Ah well, that's a long story. Why don't we all have one of your nice cups of tea and I'll tell you.'

Once they were all settled, Jonathan Higginbottom began his tale.

'What I really wanted to do after leaving university was to become a nursery nurse. You see, I just love children.' He looked at Little-Bit and grinned. 'Although, I couldn't eat a whole one.'

Little-Bit giggled nervously.

'The problem was that none of the schools I applied to could get past the whole "scary-looking alligator" thing.' He sighed and slurped his tea loudly. 'I guess it just wasn't meant to be.'

'So how did you end up working with the Resistance?' asked Rockwell.

'Well, I was as appalled as anybody by Mr White's attack on Chroma and all we hold dear, so I figured that if I couldn't get a job helping kids, the next best thing was to get a job defending our way of life. Maybe I could help the poor folk imprisoned by Mr White instead. Anyway, I applied, and Mrs M posted me to Inky Lake immediately. I suppose it was a natural fit for an

individual of
an eusuchian
persuasion.'

'I think you're
very brave,' said
Little-Bit, standing up
to give him a big hug.

'Awww, thanks.'
Jonathan Higginbottom's
eyes filled with tears. 'No
one ever hugs me.'

'So,' said Peanut.
'What's the plan? For us, I mean.'

'Well, as you know, Mr White has spies everywhere . . .'

'Yes. We've already seen some RAZERs and a couple of
the flying fish.'

'Of course you have. So you will agree that our best bet is
to travel under cover of darkness.'

'Where are we going?'

'My information is that one of my colleagues will meet
you on the Strip.'

'So, will you escort us through the forest?'

'Not through the forest. We need to take a safer route.' He
put down his mug. 'Children, you'd better scribble yourselves
something waterproof. We're going swimming.'

43
Crossing Inky Lake

espite Little-Bit's protests ('But . . . it's the best drawing I've ever done!'), Peanut and Rockwell set about erasing all traces of their camp before Jonathan Higginbottom led the group through the trees to the banks of Inky Lake. Up close, it was a sight to behold. The perfectly flat surface extended as far as the eye could see and reflected the twinkling stars and bright full moon like a vast black mirror.

'This is as good an entry point as any,' said the alligator. 'Up you get, then.'

Doodle and the three children climbed on to his giant reptilian back and sat facing forwards with their feet dangling in the cool, jet-black water. When they were all in position, Jonathan Higginbottom eased away from the bank and swam smoothly out into the vast body of the lake.

'Do you know who will be meeting us at the Strip?' asked Peanut.

'I don't, I'm afraid,' replied Jonathan Higginbottom. 'We are never told the identities of our fellow agents in case

we're ever captured. If you don't know names, you can't give people up. Mr White is not averse to using every means of, er, persuasion available to him, you see.'

'So, if you don't know who it is, how will *we* know who it is?'

'Don't worry, it will become clear. Just like when we met.'

'So, what *is* the Strip anyway?' Little-Bit was dragging her hand through the water and marvelling at how black it left her fingers. 'It sounds like it'll be fun.'

'Well, that depends on your definition of fun. If you enjoy ear-splitting noise, horrendously busy streets and panic-inducing chaos, then you'll love it.'

'Ooooh,' replied the little girl. 'That *does* sound fun!'

'Surely it would have been better to brave the Black Mountains and head straight for the Spire,' said Rockwell. 'Won't this huge detour expose us to more danger?'

'Have you ever heard of the phrase "hiding in plain sight"?' replied the alligator. 'Trust me, you will be much harder to spot among the crowds of the Strip than you would be sneaking through the Black Mountains. I can't pretend that I'm party to tactics, but in this instance, I definitely would have made the same decision. In fact, if I've learned one thing during my time with Mr and Mrs M, it's that you should always trust their judgement.'

'Jonathan Higginbottom?' It was Peanut's turn to ask a question. 'When we were flying over the valley and those two flying-fish things started to chase us, they suddenly blew up for no reason at all. Do you know what happened?'

The alligator smiled. 'I was going to talk to you about that when we got to the other side of the lake, but I suppose now is as good a time as any. My very clever colleagues in the Resistance have developed a small device that scrambles the circuits of the Exocetia – the flying fish, as you call them. Basically, you press a button and the device emits sound waves, undetectable by the human ear, that cause the Exocetia to vibrate intensely, instantly overheat and, ultimately, explode. As long as you are within one hundred metres of them and, ideally, have a clear sightline, it should work.'

'Wow!' gasped Rockwell. 'So Gavreau was right?' He noticed Peanut's confused expression. 'Oh come on, you *must* have heard of Vladimir Gavreau! The Franco-Russian scientist who experimented with weaponising infrasonic waves in the sixties? He was largely discredited by most—'

'BORING!' shouted Little-Bit.

Peanut looked at Rockwell and nodded. She turned to Jonathan Higginbottom. 'So, it was you that blew them up?'

'It was. I was watching you from the forest floor and saw

the Exocetia start to follow you. I had to wait for longer than I was totally comfortable with in order to get a good shot, but hopefully I was able to act before they managed to send further intelligence to Mr White and the RAZERs.'

'Thank you,' said Rockwell. 'Thank you so much.'

'All part of the service. Actually, I took the liberty of putting the device in the outside pocket of your rucksack, young man. It might well come in handy at some point. After all, we're depending on you.'

Rockwell blushed.

'Still want me to draw you that door?' asked Peanut.

'Hmmm. Maybe I'll stay for a bit longer after all.'

'Good show, old boy!' chirped Jonathan Higginbottom. 'Now, if I were you, I'd try and get a spot of sleep on my back there. It'll be a few hours before we reach the other side of the lake and you have a busy day ahead of you tomorrow.'

Arrival

Peanut opened her eyes and was surprised to see that it was light.

'Wh-what time is it? Where are we?' It took a few seconds for the Tetris pieces in her head to fall into place and for her to remember what had happened the night before.

'Ahh, good morning, Peanut. It's almost seven o'clock,' said Jonathan Higginbottom warmly. 'We reached the south side of the lake about two hours ago. I couldn't bring myself to wake you – you all looked so peaceful.'

Peanut looked behind her to see Little-Bit snuggled up next to Rockwell, both of them sound asleep on the alligator's back.

Doodle was standing on the bank. When he saw Peanut,

he wagged his tail and barked loudly, waking the other two.

Little-Bit yawned. 'Are we there? Have we reached the Strip?'

'Yes,' said Jonathan Higginbottom. 'It's just across there.' He pointed with his tail towards a uniform line of trees fifty metres away, beyond which they could hear the sounds of engines being revved, trams clattering along tracks and car horns beeping.

'And what do we do when we get there, exactly?' asked Rockwell, rubbing his eyes.

'Head for Main Street and turn right. It's the main avenue running through the Strip and it runs directly towards the Spire. You can't miss it. Keep a low profile, and don't do anything that might draw attention – you will need to cover all of those pens and pencils for a start, young Peanut. Somebody from the Resistance will make contact with you before you reach Rainbow Lake. You'll be in safe hands, I can promise you that.'

'Well, what are we waiting for?' said Rockwell. 'The sooner we get to the Spire, the sooner we can rescue Peanut's dad and Mr M, and the sooner we can go home. Lead the way, Señor Higginbottom . . .'

'Alas, I must leave you here. I have completed my mission and now I must return to my post. Apart from anything else, we alligators aren't really built for urban living.'

'Oh, but can't you come with us? I've never been friends with an alligator before,' pleaded Little-Bit.

'We will always be friends, regardless of whether I accompany you or not.' He nudged Little-Bit's cheek gently with his nose. 'I will remember that hug forever, little one. And I will see you again soon. I'm sure of it.'

'Thank you, Jonathan Higginbottom. For everything,' said Peanut. 'It was a pleasure to meet you. If I hear of any vacancies going at any nursery schools, I will be putting your name forward immediately.'

'That is very kind of you.'

With that, the alligator slipped under the black water and was gone.

They were on their own once more . . .

45

The Strip

eanut pulled on the cardigan that she had painted for herself as the gang walked past the row of trees. She was pleased to find that it was a good fit and, more importantly, covered the bandolier.

They found themselves at the edge of a bustling metropolis.

'That must be Main Street,' said Rockwell. 'Come on, there's a footbridge over there.'

As they crossed the raised walkway, they could see that Main Street stretched in a perfectly straight line for a couple of miles in each direction: a ten-lane artery transporting its cargo across the city, feeding dozens of smaller capillary roads on either side. Peanut remembered the instructions given to them by Jonathan Higginbottom and looked to her right. And there it was. A tall, white spike on the horizon. The heart of the city.

'The Spire,' she gasped.

'*That's* the Spire? It's miles away!' groaned Little-Bit. 'My legs are aching already!'

Alongside the wide river of traffic, a slower-moving stream of people flowed along the pavements. It was an urban canyon.

'What are those colourful shapes following everybody around?' said Rockwell. 'There's loads of them! Are they balloons?'

'I think . . .' said Peanut excitedly, 'that they're speech bubbles! Yes! Look! As people talk, whatever they say appears in type above their heads. It's like we've jumped inside a comic book!'

'That's so cool!' said Little-Bit.

Doodle barked and led them down to a raised platform at the busy roadside. A sign read: 'COURTESY TRAM: KANE PARK'. They joined the end of the queue.

In front of them stood a man wearing a stiff, beige raincoat and a yellow fedora. He was talking loudly on his phone. Rockwell looked up at the speech bubbles above his head.

'If it means taking this wise guy for a little chat down a dark alleyway, then . . .'

'Listen! I don't care how you do it, just get him to sign the papers!'

'Just close the deal, Charlie!'

Rockwell turned to Peanut and raised his eyebrows. 'How does anyone keep secrets in this town?'

'Maybe it's not a secretive kind of place,' she replied.

'Hang on a second,' said Little-Bit, looking upwards, 'Where are our speech bubbles?'

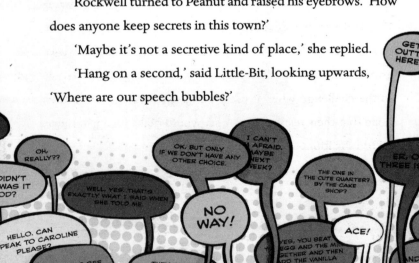

'Oh great! Yet another way for us to stand out from the crowd . . .' Rockwell sighed.

'OK. Let's just try to keep the chat to a minimum, shall we?' said Peanut, 'We don't want any unnecessary attention.'

A few minutes later, a low rumbling noise signalled the arrival of a large, chrome-trimmed burgundy tram. It looked exactly like the vintage ones that Peanut had seen on a (Melody High) school trip to the London Transport Museum a year ago. It was beautifully old-fashioned with curved glass windows at each end.

They waited patiently for passengers to get off before they boarded and claimed seats at the front of the driverless carriage. The doors slid shut and Peanut heard the crackle of electricity on the overhead lines as they pulled away.

Peanut couldn't help feeling uneasy as they headed down Main Street, directly towards the Spire. Everything was going smoothly. Too smoothly, perhaps? She was aware that since Dad had left, her default setting was one of pessimism, but nevertheless a sixth sense was telling her that trouble was just around the corner. The question was, would she be equal to the challenge when it presented itself? She hoped beyond hope that their resistance contact would make an appearance before she found out the answer.

46
'Stop, in the Name of the Law!'

Peanut, Rockwell and Little-Bit looked out of the window at the changing cityscape. The grimy grit of the fountain-pen flying buttresses and charcoal-drawn geometry of the cafes, theatres and office blocks had given way to cleaner, friendlier-looking buildings made up of thicker outlines and brighter colours. The pavements were still busy, but the people looked different. More cartoonish. Strangely, there were lots of animals, some of which were wearing clothes and walking upright!

'If this is the Strip, then what's that over there?' Little-Bit was pointing to a long line of shiny, glass high-rise buildings

in the distance to their left, running parallel to Main Street.

Peanut unfolded the map. 'Hmmm. That must be Superhero Heights.'

'Ooh, that sounds cool. Can we go there please?'

'LB, we have a mission to complete. The sooner we get to the Spire, the sooner we rescue Mr M and Dad. We don't have time for sightseeing.'

The tram slowed and came to a stop. A large, yellow speech bubble saying 'END OF THE LINE' appeared above their heads as the same words came blaring from the speakers in the ceiling.

They got off the tram.

'Right. So where now?' said Rockwell , covering his mouth as he spoke.

Peanut looked down the street. They could see the Spire much more clearly now, its razor-sharp tip reaching high into the blue sky. She could make out lots of small black squares spiralling around the outside of the white, needle-like structure. Windows, she assumed. She wondered if Dad or Mr M was looking out of one of them. Would they be lucky enough to have cells with windows?

'Jonathan Higginbottom told us to head towards the Spire. We're not far away now. Hopefully our Resistance helper will reveal themselves sooner rather than later.'

They started to walk down Main Street, which had gone down from five lanes of traffic in each direction to two. The pavements were still extremely crowded, and a continuous cloud of speech bubbles floated above the hordes expressing every emotion imaginable.

Suddenly, they became aware of a kerfuffle behind them. All four of them turned around to see an enormous, red, spiky speech bubble shoot out through the doorway of a small shop. It said 'STOP! THIEF!' in huge capital letters. It was closely followed through the door by its creator, a squat man wearing half-moon glasses and a purple waistcoat. There was broken glass all over the floor. The man was pointing directly towards them.

Seconds later, a small squirrel wearing a black mask and a stripy T-shirt came running towards them carrying a plastic bag full of something shiny. Instinctively, Peanut stuck out her leg to trip him up. As the squirrel was sent sprawling, a gold tiara flew out of the bag and rotated several times in mid-air before landing perfectly on Rockwell's head. The squirrel sat on the ground for half a second and scowled at Peanut, before springing back to his feet and disappearing into the crowd with his bag.

'There! Him! That boy with the big hair!' shouted the jeweller, pointing directly at Rockwell. 'He has the tiara! Get him!'

Rockwell looked totally bemused. '"Big hair"? Does he mean *me*?' he said to Peanut. 'How rude!'

At that moment, a small police car came hurtling around the corner with four very fat bulldogs in police uniforms inside. As it screeched to a stop at the kerb, a speech bubble came out of the loudspeaker on the vehicle's roof:

The Chase

Several of the people nearby stopped walking and turned to face the children.

'Er, Peanut . . .' said Rockwell quietly. 'What do we do now?'

Without hesitating, Peanut reached inside her cardigan and pulled the two-inch paintbrush and the thinnest marker pen from the bandolier. The crowd, seeing the illegal art materials, stepped back slightly. Quick as a flash, Peanut drew eight small circles in two rows of four on the floor. She then painted a thick black bar, big enough for the three children to stand on, across the top of them and drew a vertical line with a T-bar coming up and out of one end of it.

'Rockwell, pick up Doodle. Everyone, jump on! Hold

tight!' yelled Peanut, before kicking off and zooming down the pavement.

The makeshift scooter was surprisingly responsive, and Peanut was able to weave her way through the pedestrians with relative ease, despite a myriad of speech bubbles saying things like 'CAREFUL!' and 'WATCH OUT!' blocking her vision. She looked over her shoulder to see the police car full of bulldogs with its light flashing and the siren on. It was gaining on them.

'It's no use! They're going to catch us!' shouted Peanut. 'There's nothing else for it, we're going to have to split up!'

'What do you mean, "split up"?' replied Rockwell.

'I mean we're going to have to go in different directions.'

'Peanut, in case you'd forgotten, we're all standing on the same scooter. Remember? The one you *just painted!*'

'THIS IS THE POLICE! PULL OVER!' The bulldogs were now within a few metres of them.

'Little-Bit, can you reach the yellow pencil in my bandolier?'

'I-I think so.' She let go of Peanut's waist with one hand and managed to reach inside her cardigan with the other. 'Got it!'

'Right. Now, I want you to carefully turn around and sit down. Do it slowly. You can lean back on to my legs for stability.'

'OK. I'll try.' She turned around and sat down.

'Great!' Peanut swerved to avoid a woman walking several miniature llamas on different-coloured leads.

'Careful!' shouted Rockwell. Remember some of us are holding dogs!'

'Right. Now, LB, I want you to take the pencil, turn it around and rub out a section of the footplate. A straight line right across the middle of it.'

'But . . . won't that break it?'

'That's what I'm hoping!' She darted in between a tiger in a pinstripe suit and a woman eating some candyfloss. 'Rockwell, you like skateboarding, right?'

'Well, yes. But . . .'

'IF YOU DO NOT STOP, WE WILL BE FORCED TO SHOOT!' The police car was driving on the pavement now about five metres behind them.

'Do it, LB! Do it now!'

The little girl flipped the pencil and rubbed in a straight line as hard as she could across the middle of the footplate. The scooter split in two.

'WHOOOOOOAAAAAAAAA!'

Rockwell, with Doodle in his arms, suddenly veered sharply to the right and disappeared down an alleyway in between two doughnut shops. At the same time, Peanut and Little-Bit swerved left, straight into the road.

The police bulldogs were, understandably, confused. Two of them turned their heads to the left, following Peanut, and the other two followed Rockwell as he went right. Unfortunately for them, no one was looking straight ahead. They were heading, rather rapidly, towards a three-metre-tall model of a chocolate doughnut, covered with sprinkles and painted with the words 'STOP HERE FOR THE BEST CHOCOLATE RING ON THE STRIP'. The crash was spectacular!

Meanwhile, Peanut tried desperately to avoid the cars in the road. Luckily, there was a traffic jam, but that didn't stop the many spiky *BEEP!* speech bubbles. After a minute or so she managed to steer back on to the pavement and bring the scooter to a stop next to a bright red kiosk in the shape of an apple. The sign above said: 'CUTE FRUIT'.

Ten seconds later, Rockwell, holding Doodle in his arms, skated out from between a sushi restaurant and a launderette a few doors down the road. His head and shoulders were covered in something brown and gooey. Doodle was miraculously untouched.

'You took your time!' Peanut laughed. 'What happened?'

'We had a small incident with a vat of chilli,' replied Rockwell. 'No biggie. I'm fine.' He wiped his brow. 'Anyone else feeling a bit . . . hot?'

Little-Bit, still holding the pencil, sketched a glass of water and handed it to him, before giving Little Tail back to Peanut.

'Thanks,' he said, drinking deeply. 'So, where are we now?'

The Cute Quarter

The colours were amazing. Duck-egg blues, lime greens, fuchsia pinks and lemon yellows. This section of the Strip felt like a very happy place.

Fun, too. For a start, the shops looked exactly like the items they sold. Next to the Cute Fruit stall was a small baker's in the shape of a cupcake, complete with a towering swirl of glittery, rainbow-coloured frosting. Opposite that stood an elegant teapot cafe, painted white and pink and topped with a jolly red bow. Next to that, a honey pot with mechanical bees buzzing around its chimney, and then a giant, sleepy-looking teddy bear's head, whose yawning mouth doubled up as the door. Further down the street were giant ice creams, sunflowers, hot dogs, cacti, milk bottles and unicorns.

'Don't tell me you can actually buy a unicorn here,' scoffed Rockwell.

The characters filling the streets of this area were, again, of a very different nature to those that they'd encountered further up the road. For a start, they were nearly all either animals or walking, talking items of food. They were very simply drawn, with bold outlines and flat colours, but incredibly beautiful at the same time. They all had huge, shiny eyes, button noses and sweet smiles. There were no speech bubbles anywhere.

'Excuse me,' said Peanut to a passing frog who was wearing a rather fetching kimono. 'Can you tell me where we are? We're a little bit lost.'

'Why, of course!' he said with a heart-melting smile. 'This is the Cute

Quarter. And you are all very welcome here.'

'Of *course* it's the Cute Quarter,' whispered Rockwell.

'I think I might stay here forever,' said Little-Bit. 'Ooh, look at *her* . . .'

Across the street, in front of a two-storey pizza slice, stood the most adorable panda that the children had ever seen. She was wearing a long grass skirt, a garland around her neck comprising of pink, red and orange flowers, and a headband to match. She looked over at them with her enormous eyes and batted her ridiculously long lashes. She smiled and sashayed over.

'Why, hello there.' Her voice was smooth and sweet. 'My name is Lulu Kawaii. Do y'all need some help?'

49
Lulu Kawaii

'Lulu Kawaii? That is the *best* name!' gushed Little-Bit. 'And you are soooo beautiful.'

'Why thank you, little lady,' said the panda, grinning. 'I think you are as pretty as a peach too.' As she smiled, her tiny nose crinkled and Little-Bit giggled.

'Er, hello, Miss Kawaii,' stammered Peanut. 'We were wondering if you might know how we could get to the Rainbow Lake?'

Lulu bent down to stroke Doodle, but he backed away, tail between his legs.

'Awwww, bless your heart. Are you nervous, boy?' Her honeyed voice was soft and soothing. 'I guess I am quite big, and, well, if you haven't met a talking panda before it might take a bit of getting used to.'

As she spoke, Doodle relaxed and let her stroke him under his chin. Slowly his tail started to wag.

'There you go, fella. See? I ain't gonna hurt you.' She turned her huge eyes to Peanut. 'Now, where did you say you was headed, sweetie-pie?'

'The Rainbow Lake. We've heard that it's . . . quite a sight.'

The slightest suggestion of a frown appeared on Lulu's forehead.

'The Rainbow Lake?' she stood up. 'Heavens to Betsy, it certainly is a sight. Beautiful. Absolutely beautiful. But . . .' her eyes suddenly got even shinier, 'everything is . . . different now.'

'Can you show us how to get there?' Peanut was trying to work out ways to ask whether Lulu was their Resistance contact without actually asking if she was their Resistance contact. 'Can you . . . help us?'

The panda blinked three times.

'Well, that just dills my pickle. Of *course* I can help you. Y'all just . . . come with me.'

Peanut looked into Lulu's beautiful, black eyes. They were so big that she could see a full-length reflection of herself in them, as clear as day.

Then she noticed.

As her depth of focus adjusted, she saw a faint red pin-prick of light inside Lulu's eye, and she heard a whirring sound.

Peanut reached inside her cardigan. 'Aw, that's so kind of you, Lulu.'

'Y'all are so welcome. I'm happy to help. The Rainbow Lake is just down yonder.'

The panda turned to point down the street, and Peanut seized her opportunity.

Quick as a flash, she took her marker pen and drew a line around Lulu's ankles, circling her three times. Then she pulled the ends as hard as she could.

'Peanut! What are you doing!' shouted Little-Bit as Lulu fell forward and landed flat on her face.

'We need to get out of here! Fast!' shouted Peanut.

'Lulu! Are you OK?' said Rockwell, ignoring Peanut and running forward to help the stricken bear to her feet. 'I'm so sorry. My friend here appears to have lost her mind.'

The panda pushed herself up on to all fours and turned to face him. Rockwell jumped back in shock. Lulu's flowers were broken and strewn across her forehead. Also, her eyes were glowing bright red and looking decidedly less adorable than they had done seconds before. A small door slid open where the little, smiley mouth had been and a voice, neither soft nor soothing, bellowed, 'CODE RED! CODE RED! I HAVE LOCATED THE CONSPIRATORS!'

Then came the deafening, high-pitched sound that the children had heard before.

50

Is it a Bird?
Is it a Plane?

'This way!' shouted Peanut as she darted between the giant ice cream and the massive sunflower.

Doodle grabbed the marker-pen rope around Lulu's ankles with his teeth and tugged it hard, causing the panda to topple backwards. He then sprinted down the alleyway after the three children.

'CONSPIRATORS! HALT!' roared Lulu Kawaii. She snapped the rope and leaped to her feet with incredible speed. Then she ran after the gang.

Peanut, Rockwell, Little-Bit and Doodle dashed along a road parallel to the Strip that was paved with pink-and-yellow-chequered cake. It was soft and spongy and, after a few seconds, their cake-coated feet became heavy, making running impossible.

'Behind those bushes! Quick!' yelled Peanut. To their left was a low, pale-pink hedge. They dived behind it.

As the four of them crouched down, Peanut spotted Little-Bit grabbing a fistful of the pink shrubbery.

'Mmmm. Candyfloss!' she said, shovelling it into her mouth. Mum never normally let them have this much sugar.

'Sssh! She's coming,' said Rockwell.

Lulu Kawaii was making her way slowly up the pink and yellow path towards them. Little-Bit, seemingly unaware of the seriousness of their situation, was wolfing down the pink, wispy confectionary as if she hadn't eaten for months.

'LB. Stop,' whispered Peanut urgently.

The little girl turned to her sister, looking a little sheepish, and let out the deepest, loudest, longest burp in the history of the human digestive system.

Immediately, Lulu's red eyes swivelled towards them.

'I HAVE YOU NOW!'

Suddenly they heard a whistle from above their heads. They looked up.

'Is . . . is that a flying sideboard?' said Rockwell.

'Er, I think it might be,' replied Peanut.

Sure enough, floating a few metres above their heads

was a beautiful piece of antique furniture, made from solid walnut. On top of it, crouched in a surfing position, was a very muscular man dressed in a dark brown spandex bodystocking with a big 'TG' logo on the chest and a long, green cloak billowing out to the rear. Behind him was a levitating coffee table, a hovering dresser, a gravity-defying writing desk and a flying bedside cabinet.

'Who are *you*?' shouted Rockwell.

'Greetings citizen!' shouted the man. 'I am Table Guy! Fighting for truth, justice and a really good place to sit down and eat your dinner! Hurry! Grab a beautifully turned cabriole leg and pull yourselves up!'

51
Table Guy

Rockwell grabbed a leg and, with the help of Table Guy, hauled himself on to the sideboard. Then, between the two of them, they lifted Peanut, Little-Bit and Doodle up just before Lulu Kawaii could get to them. The furious panda snatched at their feet but she was too late.

'CODE PURPLE! CODE PURPLE!' she roared. 'THE CONSPIRATORS ARE ESCAPING!'

'By the wonder of wood!' shouted Table Guy. 'Let's fly!'

The great table train rose several metres higher into the air before rapidly soaring away from the Cute Quarter. Peanut watched, helpless, as the Spire appeared to grow smaller,

the further away they flew.

'Sorry, Dad. We were so close,' she whispered.

The five of them were crammed very tightly together on top of the sideboard. 'We can't all stay on this!' declared the muscle-bound superhero, heroically. 'We will soon start to descend! I have provided a table for each of you! Assume your positions!'

Doodle hopped across on to the bedside cabinet, Little-Bit the writing desk, Peanut the dresser and Rockwell the coffee table. They all crouched in a surfing position, as demonstrated by Table Guy.

Rockwell was smiling. "By the wonder of wood"?' He laughed. 'Is that your catchphrase?'

'It is!' Table Guy nodded, looking pleased. Every sentence he said seemed to finish with an exclamation mark.

'I'm not being funny, but were you last in the queue when they were handing out the superpowers?'

'Rockwell, don't be so rude!' shouted Little-Bit. 'Don't forget, Table Guy has just saved us.'

'The small one is correct!' said Table Guy in his deep baritone. 'That being said, you were also correct! I was very near to the end of the queue! On power-giving day, my alarm clock didn't go off and I overslept! By the time it was my turn, the cool powers – invisibility, telekinesis, shark senses – had all gone! It was either having total command over items of

furniture or being able to make really good balloon animals!
I chose tables!'

Rockwell's laughter was infectious. Soon all three children
were giggling. Even Table Guy cracked
a smile.

'Yes! It is quite funny, I suppose! But
at least I got a half-decent outfit! You
should see what Cheese Girl has to
wear! Stinky!'

'So, when did you join the
Resistance?' asked Peanut.

'Only a few weeks ago! Most of
my fellow heroes have turned a blind eye to what Mr White
has been doing over the years! They figure the worse it gets,
the more hero jobs there will be for them! But it's flawed
logic! Once the Big X hits, everything will be totally destroyed,
the residents will have to leave and there will be nothing for
anybody to protect! I just couldn't live with it any more! I
decided I had to do something!'

'So Mrs M got word to you about our mission?'

'She did!'

'So why are we flying away from the Spire?'

'You have initiated a Code Purple!' Table Guy looked
back over his shoulder. 'The panda will have photographed
your faces and by now she will have sent your picture to every

single RAZER in Chroma!
Currently, you are the four most
wanted people in town! We need to let the
heat die down!'

They were flying directly over the tall glass buildings running parallel with the Strip that they had seen from afar earlier.

'Superhero Heights,' said Peanut.

'Correct!' said Table Guy.

Far below, they saw several brightly dressed people flying, climbing, running and swinging their way through the streets.

'Look at them! Revelling in the high crime levels! What's heroic about that?' Table Guy shook his head. 'What they should really be doing is stopping crime at its root! They are cowards!'

After a few minutes, the city below them slowly started to transform into suburbia and the unlikely group began their descent. Peanut looked to her right. She saw trees. She saw ponds. She saw flowers. It looked . . . safe.

'When we land, I am going to leave you at the edge of

the Light District!' declared Table Guy. 'Peanut, you will draw disguises for your companions! You will find a safe place and rest for the night! In the morning, you will travel straight across the northern edge of the ponds and enter Vincent Fields! Look for the Yellow House! Someone will be there to meet you!'

A few minutes later, all five tables coasted towards the ground and gently touched down.

'Table Guy, I'm sorry for laughing at you,' said Rockwell. 'You are the bravest superhero I've ever met. OK, you're the only superhero I've ever met, but you're also the bravest.'

'There is no need to apologise, citizen! And there is no need to thank me either! We are on the same team!' He looked into the distance. 'Always remember . . . the great things of tomorrow arise from the ashes of today!' He looked thoughtful, his quiff blowing slightly in the wind. 'Another thing to always remember . . . once you choose hope, everything is possible!' Dramatic pause. 'Oh, and one final thing to always remember . . . while there is good and there is evil in this universe, there are also tables! And mankind will always need tables!'

He saluted, climbed aboard his sideboard, and flew off into the sunset.

'That's quite a lot of things to always remember,' said Little-Bit.

52
The Light District

he sky had turned a darker shade of blue and was infused with strokes of gold, orange and lilac. As Peanut, Rockwell, Little-Bit and Doodle followed the flamingo-pink path that led into the Light District, they marvelled at their beautiful surroundings. Buttery daffodils lined their route through a mauve latticework of shadows cast by the poplar trees shielding them from view. A small platoon of bumblebees provided the quiet, humming soundtrack. It was hard to believe that just a couple of hours ago they had been in the midst of the noisy chaos of the Strip.

They walked for half an hour until they reached a large

field spattered with bright-red poppies. Tired and hungry, they sat down in the long grass. Peanut pulled Little Tail from her bandolier and quickly drew some sausage rolls that tasted faintly of liquorice. 'Don't worry. I'll do my best to paint us something more delicious in the morning,' she promised.

Once they had eaten, she set about drawing disguises for everybody. She chose simple farmer's outfits, complete with wide-brimmed straw hats, so they would blend into the scenery and keep their faces hidden.

They were just getting into their new gear when Doodle suddenly sat bolt upright and looked back towards the path. 'Everybody quiet,' hissed Rockwell. 'Get down.'

They flattened themselves against the earth and peered through the long grass as six tall, silver figures emerged from behind the poplar trees and glided silently along the path. Little-Bit gasped. Peanut and Rockwell both covered her mouth. Yes, they were tall, and yes, they were fast, but it was the fact that the RAZERs made no noise whatsoever that was the scariest thing. It was obviously a key part of their design –

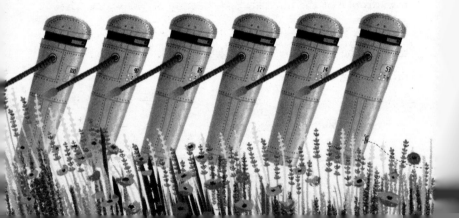

after all, stealth was imperative when capturing fugitives – but silence wasn't something Peanut would ever have thought of as particularly frightening. Until now.

The four friends collectively held their breath as the robots glided within a few metres of them. It was only when they disappeared behind the haystacks and over the hill that the children were finally able to breathe.

'That was too close!' panted Rockwell. 'What are we going to do?'

'We need to keep moving,' replied Peanut.

Carefully, she stood up and looked around. She noticed that the poppy field they were hiding in sloped down to the banks of a large pond. She ran down the hill for a closer look and saw that it was connected, via a network of canals, to a series of other ponds.

She had an idea.

She took Little Tail from her bandolier and drew a long wiggly line with a sharp hook on the end. She then whirled it around her head a few times like a lasso and threw it towards one of the huge lily pads floating on the water. The hook pierced the surface and Peanut pulled hard, dragging it towards the bank. She then took her block of charcoal and drew a long, thick pole.

'OK. Everybody on,' she said.

'Ooh, this is just like *The Tale of Mr. Jeremy Fisher!*' said Little-Bit, beaming as she scrambled on board.

Once they were all sitting comfortably, Peanut stood up with the pole, lowered one end into the water until it hit the bottom, and pushed off. They drifted effortlessly out into the middle of the pond.

As they quietly cut through the water, Peanut was able to steer with the pole, guiding them towards the narrow canal on the southern side of the pond. The sun set as they cut an elegant swathe through the beautiful russets and purples reflected in the surface. Rockwell's eyelids felt heavy. Little-Bit and Doodle were already asleep.

'Go on. Catch some Zzzs,' said Peanut as she guided them underneath a green wooden bridge spanning the canal. 'I'll wake you when we reach Vincent Fields.'

Starry Night

By the time Peanut had steered them to the far side of the final pond, night had fallen. The sky, sketched in several shades of dark blue, appeared to move and swirl with the breeze, ebbing and flowing around a beautifully composed canvas studded with large, yellow stars. The dappled, sun-flecked terrain of the Light District had given way to the harder lines and more distinct brushstrokes of Vincent Fields.

Peanut looked to their right. She could see a small town, half a mile or so away, silhouetted against the brilliant sky. The few splashes of cosy, warm orange in the windows of the houses suddenly made her miss the comforts of home. And Mum.

'That looks like as good a place as any to start looking for the Yellow House,' she said to herself. 'The sooner we find it, the sooner we can bed down for the night.'

She gently woke the others and they set off across the fields, following the paths cut into the corn. Eventually they arrived at a flat, dusty road that led into the town.

It didn't take long for them to find the Yellow House, despite the fact that there were no streetlights. It certainly lived up to its name! The small cottage was on the corner of the first block of buildings they came to and, compared to the buildings surrounding it, it was luminous.

It didn't look like anybody was home. The green shutters were all closed and, although the cottage itself shone, there was no light coming from inside. Peanut strode confidently forward and knocked on the door. Nothing. She knocked again. Still nothing.

'Oh, Peanut. I'm so tired. Please can we just go back to sleep?' pleaded Little-Bit.

Peanut was tired too. She tried the door handle and, to her surprise, it opened.

'Great. Come on.'

'Er, I think this is what's known as "breaking and entering",' said Rockwell.

'Yes, I suppose it is,' said Peanut, before kicking off her boots and disappearing inside, closely followed by Little-Bit and Doodle.

Rockwell shrugged and followed them.

The front door led straight into a sitting room, sparsely furnished with a few simple wood and wicker chairs, a couple of old crates that doubled up as tables and a green spiral staircase in the corner. The floor was covered with large terracotta tiles that felt nice and cool against the children's tired feet.

On one of the chairs sat an envelope with a large letter P printed on it. Peanut picked it up and opened it.

Peanut Jones.

At daybreak, head to Die Brücke. Stay close to the city limits. You will be met at the beginning.

Agent X

'Met at the beginning?' said Rockwell. 'The beginning of what?'

'I guess we'll find out,' sighed Peanut. 'More importantly, I wonder who Agent X is.'

'We don't have to leave until daybreak? So does that mean we can go to sleep?' said Little-Bit.

'Yes,' said Peanut, relieved that they were in the right place and back on track. 'Head upstairs and see if you can find a bed.'

At the top of the stairs was a small bathroom and a bedroom containing three small but comfortable-looking beds and a dog basket. The children washed their faces and climbed in.

Despite their exhaustion, all three struggled to sleep.

'Peanut . . .' said Little-Bit after a couple of minutes. 'I wish Daddy was here. He would love this city.'

Then, after another minute, 'Do you think we'll ever find him?'

'You're right,' said Peanut. 'He would love it here.' Her eyes prickled. 'And yes, I do think we're going to find him. I can feel it in my bones.'

'Whenever I couldn't get to sleep, he would always sing me songs. Peanut, will you sing to me now?'

'You know I can't, LB. My voice is awful. It would give you nightmares.'

'Oh pleeeeeaaaase, Peanut. Just a nursery rhyme or something.'

'Just close your eyes LB and—'

'Twinkle, twinkle, little star . . .'

A clear, sweet voice from the other side of the room started to sing.

' . . . How I wonder what you are.

Up above the world so high

Like a diamond in the sky.

Twinkle, twinkle, little star,

How I wonder what you are.'

'Rockwell,' Little-Bit yawned. 'I'm beginning to like you.'

Within a minute they were all asleep.

54
Vincent Fields

The beams from the rising sun cut through the green slats in shards, painting dramatic, stripy shadows across the three children. Little-Bit had been the first to wake. Now she hopped out of bed, stroked a stretching Doodle and opened the shutters. It was already a beautiful morning. The cornfields that they had walked across the night before were resplendent in a host of buttery yellows and golds, and the red road leading out of town cut through them like a hot knife. A murder of crows took off noisily from the fields, flocking in anticipation of an early morning hunt.

'Peanut! Rockwell! Get up! It's morning.'

They breakfasted on fried eggs that Peanut painted as carefully as she could using her watercolours.

'They look great,' said Rockwell, 'They don't taste of fried eggs – more like some sort of mild goat's cheese – but they *look* great.'

After they'd eaten, they gathered their things and left the Yellow House. They walked down the deserted red road and back across the cornfields until they reached the curtain of poplar trees that marked the outskirts of the city. From there they turned right and followed the road.

As they walked, the sun rose in the sky, causing the children to swelter underneath their straw hats. In contrast, the sunflowers filling the fields basked in the heat, turning their faces to soak up as much Vitamin D as possible. The children were very grateful for the temporary shade the trees provided and tried to linger there for as long as possible, but Doodle, seemingly oblivious to the heat, drove them on relentlessly, turning to bark whenever they stopped.

As the sun reached its highest point, they sat underneath a blossoming almond tree, chatting while they ate some lunch (spray-painted hot cross buns that tasted vaguely of turnip).

'So Peanut,' said Little-Bit, her mouth full of turnipy bread, 'which school do you think I'd like best when I'm older? Melody High or St Hubert's?'

'Melody High,' said Peanut firmly. 'Everyone loves it there and St Hubert's is like a kind of prison.'

'Oh, come on, Peanut,' said Rockwell. 'There must be *something* you like about St Hubert's.'

'Er . . . I like home time.'

'You know what I mean. Surely you've learned something interesting since you've been there?'

'She's met you,' chirped Little-Bit, causing two faces to redden. 'I think she's pretty pleased about that!'

'Be quiet and eat, LB!' snapped Peanut, but she didn't disagree with her little sister.

'Well,' continued Peanut, 'I suppose the fact that you knew how to design that hang-glider was pretty cool. I wouldn't mind learning how to do something like that.'

'Yes! I knew it!' enthused Rockwell. 'When we get back, I'll lend you this ace book I've got. It's called *Aerospace Engineering and the Principles of Flight*. Two thousand fun-packed pages of kinematics, dynamics and propulsion. You're going to love it!'

Peanut and Little-Bit looked at each other and laughed.

'One more question,' said Rockwell, suddenly looking a bit more serious. 'What happens once we've rescued Mr M and your dad?'

'Well, I guess we take Mr M back to Mrs M, and then we go home. Mum will be so pleased to see Dad when she realises that he didn't desert us after all. And everything will be OK again. I'll go back to Melody H—' She stopped herself from finishing the sentence.

'Ah, yes, of course. You'll go back to Melody High –' Rockwell sighed – 'and I'll be happy for you.' He smiled. 'I mean it. I'll miss you though. It's been cool having someone to hang out with, even if it is usually at a distance of five metres.'

Peanut had been so determined not to make any friends at St Hubert's that she hadn't ever considered why Rockwell had been so keen to be her study buddy in the first place. She suddenly realised it was because he was lonely. Rockwell was more than clever enough for St Hubert's, but he didn't fit in with the other kids any more than Peanut did.

She smiled.

'Rockwell. We're friends now. That's not going to change, regardless of which schools we go to. Anyway, you never know. Maybe you'll decide to go to Melody High one day. I think you'd like it.'

55
Captured

The rest of the afternoon passed without incident, something that they were all thankful for.

After a couple of hours, they arrived at a long, white wooden fence that ran in a perfectly straight line towards the centre of the city. The rolling hills, brimming with flowers, trees and crops, all stopped suddenly and with precision at the boundary. On the other side of the fence was water. A lot of water. A huge expanse, perfectly still, like a horizontal mirror.

A few metres from them was a tall signpost, similar to the one that Peanut had seen back in the North Draw.

'Die Bruk?' shouted Little-Bit looking up at the sign. 'What's a Die Bruk?'

'You pronounce it "Dee Brooker",' said Rockwell. 'It's German for "The Bridge".'

'Great! Let's swim to the bridge then,' said Little-Bit gleefully.

Rockwell groaned. 'I hate swimming.'

'We won't have to swim,' said Peanut. 'Look.'

To their left were several small, woodblock-print rowing boats tied to a jetty. They jumped over the fence and climbed into the first boat.

'Leave this to me. I did canoeing in the Cubs once,' said Rockwell proudly. 'Peanut, please would you unhitch the rope.'

After several failed attempts at launching (it took him a while to remember that the rower shouldn't be facing forwards), Rockwell eventually started pulling the boat through the water. The lake was huge, extending out past the city limits to their left, and almost as far as the Spire to their right.

Peanut lifted her hand to shield her eyes from the bright red glow of the swirling, angry-looking sky. She noticed that she was shaking. She felt nervous, but wasn't sure why. They could see the bridge more clearly now: a simple structure interrupted by windowless double-height towers every hundred metres or so. At its left-hand end, a wide set of stairs led down to a small, grassy island, attached to which was another jetty.

'It's the beginning,' said Peanut while scanning the area for their Resistance contact. 'The beginning of the bridge that

leads directly to the Spire.'

A couple of minutes later they arrived at the island and hitched the boat to a post. It was only when they walked up the stairs and were standing at the end of the bridge that they noticed that the towers weren't, in fact, entirely windowless. Each one had a small opening near the top, and a door at the bottom, facing back along the length of the bridge. And at each window stood a RAZER.

The RAZER in the nearest tower was looking straight at the four new arrivals on the bridge. Its eyes instantly

changed from green to red. Then, with alarming speed, it disappeared from the top window, reappeared at the door and zoomed silently towards them. Instinctively Peanut scooped up Little-Bit, and Rockwell grabbed Doodle, but before they had a chance to formulate a plan, the robot was upon them.

'CODE RED! CODE RED! I HAVE LOCATED THE CONSPIRATORS!' it bellowed. As quick as a flash, two metal arms extended around either side of the group, forming a loop, which then rapidly contracted, pulling the foursome tight against the robot's body and lifting their feet off the floor. Then a little door opened up on its side and four thin cables shot out and attached themselves to the prisoners' ankles. They were well and truly captured.

'RAZER 72 CALLING ALL UNITS . . . I HAVE THE

CONSPIRATORS . . . TRANSPORTING THEM TO SECTOR 1 IMMEDIATELY!'

The robot then spun 180 degrees on the spot, and started to glide, at speed, along the bridge towards the Spire.

'Er, what just happened?' said Rockwell, trying not to sound scared.

'We blew it, that's what' Peanut sighed, glancing nervously up at the Spire. 'After everything we've been through, we blew it.'

Little-Bit looked up at RAZER 72. 'Hello, Mr Robot. Where are you taking us?'

It didn't reply. It just kept hurtling along the bridge, past tower after tower. Peanut noticed two green lights in every window turn to red as they approached, and all of a sudden, her head started to ache. She put her hands to her temples and wondered how she'd got into this mess. *This is it*, she thought. *I've let everybody down.*

She felt like screaming.

56
The Long Walk

As they passed yet another tower, RAZER 72 suddenly slowed before coming to a complete stop.

'CONSPIRATORS! MY CHARGE LEVELS ARE LOW! YOU WILL NOW WALK IN FRONT OF ME!'

'All right, pal, turn the volume down,' said Rockwell as the ankle ties were released and the gripping arms were loosened so that they could walk along the bridge.

'Where are we going?' asked Peanut, 'To the Spire? Are you putting *us* in prison too?'

Still the robot didn't reply.

'Tell me, why exactly do you and your kind hate creativity so much? What's wrong with a little freedom of expression?

What's wrong with a little colour?'

The robot stopped and turned its glowing red eyes to Peanut. She was surprised to see that even though they were entirely mechanical, they carried a resigned, sad expression.

72's metallic voice sounded softer. 'Listen to me, little girl, you must do exactly as I say.'

'Why should I?!' she shouted.

'Please keep your voice down,' the RAZER said. 'You will draw unnecessary attention to us.'

'GOOD! I *WANT* TO DRAW UNNECESSARY ATTENTION TO US! It would be nice to be able to *draw* anything, quite frankly! And how dare you tell me what to do! Of all the— Hang on. Did you just say . . . "please"?'

'I did.'

'But . . . you're an evil RAZER. Evil RAZERs don't have manners.'

'As I was saying, it is in your interest to do exactly as I say. Please, will you do that?'

Once again, Peanut was thrown by the 'please'.

'And, as I was saying, why should I?'

'Because it's your only hope of completing your mission successfully.'

Rockwell gasped. Peanut's mouth fell open. Little-Bit grinned.

'M-my mission? What do you know about my mission?'

'I know everything about your mission. I have been fully briefed.'

'Whoa! You're in the Resistance?' shouted Little-Bit.

'You're Agent X?' said Rockwell.

'CONSPIRATORS!' the RAZER's old voice had returned. 'YOU WILL BE SILENT! WALK!'

The three children looked at each other. Doodle's tail twitched. They started to walk.

'You must look straight ahead at all times,' said 72 quietly. 'And it would be beneficial if you were to look a bit more . . . afraid. I can only give you information when we are in between towers. We cannot arouse suspicion.'

'So . . . you're an undercover agent?' asked Peanut.

'Affirmative.'

'But . . . weren't you built by Mr White?'

'Affirmative.'

'So . . . why are you acting against him?'

'I am a second-generation RAZER – a considerable upgrade on the launch model. We have been given more autonomy by the programmers. We have the ability to weigh up a situation and act as we see fit with no need for instruction. We can make decisions. So, when I saw what was happening to Chroma and its citizens, I made a decision to act.'

'So you approached Mr and Mrs M?'

'I received an all-unit call when Malcolm Markmaker was captured. I made sure I was part of the platoon that brought him in.' 72's eyes flickered blue before returning to red. 'I was guarding him on the Strip and I spotted an opportunity to explain my situation to him. It is to his great credit that he believed me and trusted me enough to inform me of a line of contact to Millicent Markmaker.'

They passed another tower.

'When I got in touch with her to offer my services,' continued 72 a few minutes later, 'she also believed me. She said I was her most powerful weapon. It made me feel . . . proud.' They were approaching another tower. 'FASTER, CONSPIRATORS!' bellowed 72. The children looked suitably forlorn, while Doodle walked with his tail between his legs.

When they had passed the tower, Rockwell looked up at the robot.

'So, since you've been with the Resistance, what have you done to help bring down Mr White?'

'Nothing,' replied 72.

'Nothing?' said Rockwell. 'Brilliant.'

'I have only ever had three directives from Millicent Markmaker. The first was to gather as much intelligence as possible while going about my regular duties. I was told to act normally until such time as I received my second directive.'

'And what was that?' asked Peanut.

'To make sure I was in the first security tower on Die Brücke when three children and a dog arrived.'

'And the third?'

72 turned its red eyes to Peanut. 'To get the four of you into the Spire.'

57

The Cipher

You're going to get us into the Spire?' said Peanut. 'How?'

'We are going to walk straight in,' said 72. 'As far as the other RAZERs are concerned, you are my prisoners. No one will challenge us.'

'And what do we do once we're in there?'

'You will need to locate Malcolm Markmaker's cell, set him free and escape.'

'And what about my dad?' asked Peanut.

'I'm afraid I know nothing of any *dad*,' replied 72. 'Maybe Malcolm Markmaker will be able to help you with that.'

Peanut nodded.

'But how on earth will we find Mr M?' said Rockwell.

'Look at the size of the tower!'

'Rockwell has got a point,' said Peanut. 'Aren't there more than a thousand cells? How will we know which one Mr M is in?'

'I have gathered a piece of information to help you with that.'

Another small door on the robot's body opened and a mechanical arm came out holding a piece of paper. Peanut took it.

```
         Fathom
  AERLT  MKOEN  KFITT
  AOCEO  MLXWW  RRSLY
```

'I don't understand. What does it mean?'

'All prisoner locations are encrypted for security reasons. This is the cipher for the location of Malcom Markmaker's cell.'

'What's a cipher?'

'It's a secret code,' said Little-Bit, who was looking at the piece of paper over Peanut's shoulder. 'I love secret codes.'

'So it's a puzzle?' asked Peanut.

'Well, it's *obviously* an anagram,' interrupted Rockwell. 'Anyone can see that.'

'Can they?'

'Yes. Give me a minute or two and I'll work it out . . .'

Little-Bit shook her head. 'I don't think it's as simple as an anagram. Why is the word "Fathom" not in capital letters?'

'It's telling us to fathom out the anagram, of course!' snapped Rockwell. 'Now, be quiet. I need to concentrate.'

'There is no time,' said 72 coming to a sudden stop. 'We have reached our destination. And there is a problem.'

58

The Rainbow Lake

he wooden bridge led straight on to a wide expanse of featureless white concrete which surrounded the most extraordinary thing that the children had ever seen in their lives: a perfectly circular body of multicoloured water, about a mile in diameter. The Rainbow Lake. 'Whoa!' said all three children as they approached the edge. It was a breathtaking sight, so beautiful that it almost didn't seem real.

The lake was made up of seven concentric circles of colour, each clearly defined and not blending with the one next to it. The outside ring was red, the next orange, then yellow, then green, then blue, then indigo and finally violet. It looked like a multicoloured running track made of water.

'Incredible,' purred Peanut.

In the middle of the lake was a small island, ringed by a tall fence made out of giant crayons. The majority of the fence was painted white, but there were large sections where the crayons' colour was still visible. Peanut assumed it was in the process of being whitewashed. Dotted all around the fence were more watchtowers, similar to those on the bridge, each with a window containing the glowing green eyes of a RAZER.

Directly opposite where the children were standing, on

the other side of the water, reaching high into the air, was what looked like a vertical section of the bridge they'd just walked across. At its base was a huge wheel connected by a series of cogs to a handle.

'Look at all those drawbridges,' said Rockwell. Sure enough, there were several that ran around the perimeter of the crayon fence. 'One for each district, I bet.'

Just beyond the crayon fence, however, was the main event. The soaring, white tower that was the Spire. It was studded with a spiral of small black windows that followed the taper of the massive spike to a perfect point 500 metres above their heads.

From this close, it seemed even bigger than Peanut had imagined. And the task of finding Mr M seemed more daunting than ever.

'So, what's the problem?' whispered Peanut.

72 made a strange clicking noise. 'We might have to revise our plan to walk into the Spire,' it said quietly. 'It is impossible. Security has been tightened and the drawbridges have been raised, therefore we are unable to make our way across the Rainbow Lake via the drawbridges.'

'So, what do we do?' said Rockwell, a note of panic in his voice.

'We must revert to Plan B,' said 72 softly. 'Peanut Jones. Listen very carefully. When I say "go" I want you to push me into the Rainbow Lake and then all of you must dive in after me.'

'Dive in?' spluttered Rockwell, clearly alarmed. 'But I hate swimming!'

'*Sssshhhhh!*' said both Peanut and Little-Bit.

'B-but the thing is, I can't actually swim,' he said quietly.

Doodle looked up at Rockwell, wagged his tail and barked.

'Don't worry. I think he's saying that he'll help you,' said Peanut. 'Just hold on to Doodle once you've jumped in.'

'Oh, well that's all right then,' said Rockwell, still not looking convinced. 'I'll just cling on to the drawing of the dog and everything will be fine.'

72 spoke quickly and precisely. 'Once you are in the lake, you will need to swim underwater directly across to the island. On the concrete wall, approximately two metres below the surface, you will see an opening. It is an access point for a colour-correction filter. It has not been used for a long time but the infrastructure is still intact. Swim through the opening and it will lead to a disused facility room. From there you will be able to use the computer terminal to locate the right cell and access the main part of the building via the elevator. To find which cell you require you will need to unscramble the code I have given you.'

'Can't you help us do that?' asked Peanut.

'I'm afraid not. My programming doesn't cover code work. Does that all make sense, Peanut Jones?'

'Er, yes. I-I think so,' she replied. 'And what will happen to you?'

'A RAZER is not designed to be submerged in water. My circuits will be flooded and I will cease to function.'

'You'll . . . you'll die?'

'Affirmative.'

'What?' said Little-Bit. 'But I don't want you to die!'

'There must be another way,' said Peanut.

'There is no other way,' said the robot. 'The other RAZERs will be distracted by my falling into the Rainbow Lake and it will give you the time to make it to the filter opening. It must be done.'

'But it's so unfair!' sobbed Little-Bit.

'Little girl. You must remember that I have lived my whole life for this moment. For me, it is an honour. If my final act can help to save the city of Chroma, then I will die a happy robot.' Its eyes flashed to green as it looked at her. 'Now. Are you all ready?'

'Can you shield me from view for one minute?' said Peanut. She reached inside her farmer's shirt and pulled out the pencil. She sketched four diving-masks and plucked them out of the air. She handed one each to Rockwell and Little-Bit, and pulled a mask over Doodle's eyes.

Rockwell looked terrified. 'So we're actually doing this?'

'Yes,' said Peanut. 'Little-Bit, when we jump in the water, put your arms around my shoulders. OK?'

'OK,' she sniffed.

'YOU THERE! RAZER 72! STATE YOUR BUSINESS!' The voice came from the watchtower on the other side of the lake near the drawbridge.

'It's time,' said 72. 'Go!'

'Deep breath, everyone!' said Peanut as she pushed 72 as hard as she could. The robot toppled over into the water. As it fell, it looked back at Peanut. Its eyes were glowing bright green. She whispered, 'Thank you.'

Peanut saw the first of the sparks fly before she, Little-Bit, Rockwell and Doodle followed RAZER 72 into the red water. The masks worked brilliantly, and, despite everything being shades of crimson, she could see perfectly. With Little-Bit on her back, she frog-kicked as hard as she could through the water and was pleased when her surroundings changed first to orange and then to yellow. She looked back to see Doodle gamely swimming through the amber water with Rockwell clinging tightly to his midriff. They swam from yellow to green to blue to indigo before finally reaching violet. And there it was. An opening in the concrete wall of the lake, about a metre wide and fifty centimetres tall. Peanut took Little-Bit from her back and pushed her through the filter first. Then she made sure Doodle and Rockwell made it before swimming through after them.

Once she had squeezed through the opening, she found herself being pulled along by a very strong current within the chute. It was like riding a waterslide except that she was entirely underwater. After ten seconds of twisting and turning, her head broke the surface and she gasped for air.

59
The Spire

s Peanut got her breath back she looked around. She had surfaced in a small round pool of purple water. Little-Bit and Rockwell were lying on the dirty concrete floor, breathing heavily. They had, like Peanut, lost their farmer disguises. Doodle, meanwhile, was sniffing at the bottom of a metallic door in the far corner.

Peanut pulled herself out of the pool and shivered. Little-Bit looked at her. 'Poor 72,' she said sadly. 'It was the bravest robot I have ever met.'

'It certainly was,' agreed Peanut. 'Another reason to rescue Dad and Mr M. We can't let 72's sacrifice be for nothing. Rockwell, any luck with that code?'

'I just almost drowned! Give me a chance!' He pulled the piece of slightly damp paper from his rucksack and started looking at it intently.

In the corner opposite the door was a small desk with a computer terminal on it. Little-Bit walked over and started tapping away on the keyboard.

'I don't think they'll have Minecraft,' said Rockwell, smiling.

'Very funny,' said Little-Bit. 'OK, I've found a map of the building. Every floor and every cell is numbered and I would guess that this door leads into elevator shaft E3 which gives us direct access to the prison floors. All we need is Mr M's cell number.'

Peanut shook her head. Sometimes it was hard to believe that her sister was only five.

'So, Mr Codebreaker, we're all waiting for you.'

'Well, it's got to be an anagram,' said Rockwell. 'I just can't work out why it's in blocks of five letters.'

Fathom
AERLT MKOEN KFITT
AOCEO MLXWW RRSLY

Little-Bit stood up from the chair by the computer and walked over.

'Don't you think that "Fathom" is a keyword?' she said to Rockwell.

'I told you, "fathom" means "work out". It's just telling us to work it out.'

'Why would they do that? They don't actually want us to work it out, do they?'

Rockwell looked at her. He realised that she was right. How annoying.

'OK, what do you mean by "keyword"?'

'Well, in my *Junior Puzzler*, there are often keywords that act as the cipher that cracks the code.'

'Of course!' said Rockwell. 'A cipher! A word that will, somehow, make sense of all the other letters. But how does "fathom" do that, clever clogs?'

'Well, it could do it in lots of different ways. Sometimes it *is* a literal clue, other times it's all to do with sequencing.'

'What's sequencing?' asked Peanut.

'Duh. The order in which you read the letters.'

Little-Bit took the piece of paper from Rockwell and stared at it for a full thirty seconds.

'Wait a minute . . . It couldn't be that simple, could it?'

'What?' asked Rockwell nervously.

'Yes! I knew it! It's a columnar transposition cipher!'

'It's a *what*?' said Rockwell. 'Now you're just making up words!'

'No, I'm not! It's a columnar transposition cipher!' She started to bounce with happiness.

'Oh no, please don't dance,' said Rockwell. 'Just explain what a communal transfiguring siren is.'

'It'll be easier to show you. Peanut, can I borrow your pencil? Right. Let's start with our keyword, "Fathom" . . .' She wrote it down.

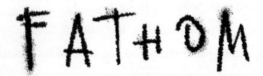

'Now, if we were to assign each letter a number, from 1 to 6, depending on where it sits alphabetically, we would end up with this . . .'

'OK. Now let's add our mysterious blocks of letters. We'll put the first block of five, A, E, R, L and T in column "1" . . .'

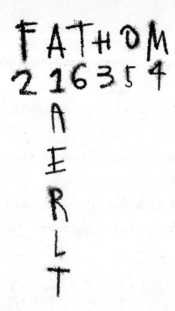

'Next, let's add the next block, M, K, O, E and N in column
2 . . .'

F A T H O M
2 1 6 3 5 4
M A
K E
O R
E L
N T

FATHOM
2 16 3 5 4
MARKMA
KERFLO
ORSIXC
ELLTWE
NTYTWO

'I still don't get it,' said Rockwell, puzzled.

'I do!' said Peanut. 'LB, you're a *genius*!'

'Can someone please explain?' said a forlorn Rockwell.

'It's so easy once you see it!' Peanut beamed. 'Just read across, line by line, left to right.'

'MARKMA, KERFLO, ORSIXC, ELLTWE, NTYTWO. What does *that* mean?'

'Write it down. Come on, you're meant to be the smart one.'

Rockwell took the pencil.

MARKMAKERFLOORSIXCELLTWENTYTWO

And then he saw it. 'Markmaker. Floor six. Cell twenty-two.'

Rockwell looked at Little-Bit, shook his head and held up his hand. 'OK. That is pretty smart. I admit it. You *are* a genius, Little-Bit. High five.'

'All in a day's puzzling.' she replied cheerily, slapping Rockwell's palm. 'Now, let's work out how to get to floor six, cell twenty-two.'

The Rescue

The drawings took her a long time. Peanut was determined to get them just right – after all, every detail had to be accurate for this to work. But it was hard when you were relying on memory.

'No, they're definitely taller than that,' said Little-Bit.

'She's right,' agreed Rockwell. 'And the glowing eyes are a bit bigger.'

Peanut was using every item in the bandolier to draw the two RAZERs. The main body was made up of several layers of watercolour, the arms were sketched with charcoal and the details were all added with Little Tail.

'Make sure you paint the eyes green,' said Little-Bit. 'I liked it best when 72's eyes were green.'

Eventually, she finished and stepped back to admire her work.

'Peanut, you're *so* clever,' said Rockwell.

'You're the best artist ever!' agreed Little-Bit. 'They're *so* good!'

Peanut nodded. 'They're not bad, are they? Let's hope they do the trick.'

Peanut and Rockwell stepped into the bottom halves of their RAZER costumes, picked up Doodle and Little-Bit, put them on their shoulders and then put the top halves on.

'I hope nobody notices our feet,' said Rockwell anxiously.

'I'm sure it'll be fine. As long as we move quickly and efficiently.'

Peanut shuffled over towards the lift door and pressed the button. When it arrived, Little-Bit reached out through an armhole and pressed the button marked '6'. The doors slid shut and the lift started moving upwards.

Seconds later, it stopped and the doors opened to reveal a long, arcing corridor with identical doors on either side every two metres or so. It reminded Peanut of her mother's office. Each door had a number stencilled on it in black, odd numbers on the left, even on the right.

Peanut and Rockwell started to walk as smoothly as possible down the corridor – easier said than done when (a) you have a small child/dog on your shoulders, and (b) the eyeholes in your costume don't quite line up with your eyes.

'Little-Bit,' whispered Rockwell. 'Can you read the numbers on the doors?'

'Yes,' she replied. 'Keep going. We're up to number four.'

A minute or so later they arrived at their destination.

'Here it is,' said Little-Bit. 'And the coast is clear.'

Quickly, Little-Bit lifted the head from her costume and jumped down from Rockwell's shoulders. Rockwell helped Peanut and Doodle out of theirs. Peanut grabbed a marker pen from her bandolier and drew a small keyhole on the door.

Then, in the air in front of her and using the same pen, she drew a key. She picked up the key, put it in the keyhole and turned it. The door sprang open.

Sure enough, standing inside cell twenty-two was the man that she recognised from the gilt-framed photograph in Mrs M's sitting room. It was Malcolm Markmaker.

But, unfortunately for Peanut and her friends, he wasn't alone.

Part Four

...in which Peanut finds
herself in a spot of bother

(well, several spots of bother, actually)

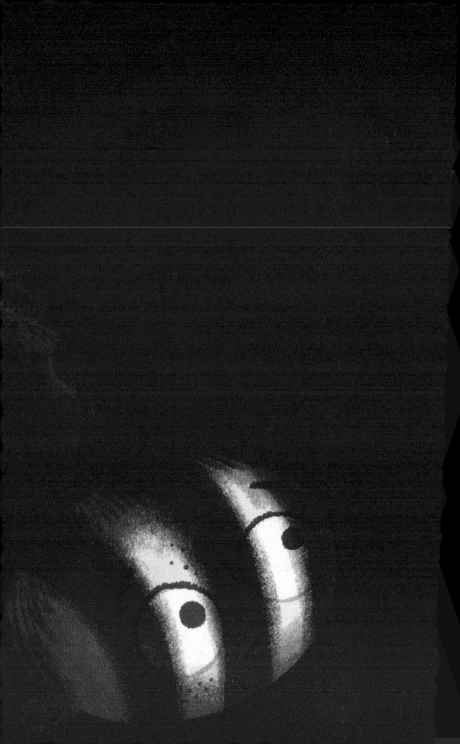

61
Alan

Peanut opened her eyes to find herself in almost total darkness and lying on something cold and hard. She sat up.

It was impossible to see anything, but she could hear breathing. Someone was in the room with her.

'Rockwell? LB? Doodle?'

'They're not here, I'm afraid,' said a deep, gravelly voice.

Then it all came back to her.

When they had opened the door to Mr Markmaker's cell, they had found him standing next to a very tall, very muscular man whose pale face was spattered with orange freckles that matched his hair. Upon seeing them, he had pulled on a mask to cover his nose and mouth, and sprayed them with

something. The next thing she knew was when she woke up in darkness.

'Who are you?' she said.

'You don't need to know my name,' he replied. 'You just need to answer my questions.'

'Where am I? Where are the others?'

'You and your friends are safe. For now.'

'Are you Mr White?'

'No. But I am the next best thing. I am his most trusted lieutenant.' Peanut could hear the pride in his voice.

'Are you the big ginger bloke who was in Mr M's cell?'

'My hair is auburn, actually. But . . . yes.'

'And your name is . . . ?'

'Why are you so interested in my name?' There was a slight note of irritation in the man's voice now.

'Why won't you tell me what it is? Are you embarrassed by it?' said Peanut. 'Is it Bumface or something?'

'No! It's . . . it's . . . well, it's Alan, if you must know.' She heard him stand up. 'Anyway, I'm the one asking the questions here!'

'Well, technically, I'm actually the one asking questions.'

'Well, you shouldn't be!'

'Why not?' replied Peanut.

'That's another question!'

'Is it?'

'STOP!'

Peanut heard Alan sit back down.

'Miss Jones,' he said. 'How did you come to be in Chroma?'

'Ah, that'd be telling.'

'We have seized your contraband drawing materials. There's no way you could have brought them through any of the known portals without us being aware of it. So you must have arrived via another avenue.'

Peanut's hand involuntarily went to her right hip. Just before they had left the facilities room in their RAZER costumes, she had painted a small pocket into her dungarees and hidden Little Tail inside. The pencil was the one thing she couldn't afford to lose. Not if she ever wanted to get back home.

Click.

Suddenly, the room was flooded with bright white light. Peanut covered her face with her hands and closed her eyes tightly. A few seconds later she opened them to find Alan's face just centimetres from hers.

'Is there anything else that you are withholding from us . . . *little girl*?' he growled, coating the last two words with a particularly potent venom.

'No, *Alan!*' she replied, trying to sound equally as poisonous.

Alan stepped back and fiddled with the headset he was wearing.

Peanut seized the opportunity to have a quick look around the room. It was tiny – about three metres by two metres. She was sitting on a concrete bench at one end. Above her head was a small barred window, open to the elements, through which she could see bright, twinkling stars against a dark purple sky. At the opposite end of the cell was a chair, behind which was a heavily secured door. Directly above that was a small TV screen. The rest of the room was entirely devoid of decoration, except for some huge black type printed on the right-hand wall that read 'F99-C42'.

Floor ninety-nine, cell forty-two, thought Peanut.

Suddenly, the screen came to life in a burst of brilliant white before fading out to reveal a silhouette of a man's head

and shoulders. He was wearing a white fedora hat pulled down low over his eyes.

'Mr White . . .' whispered Peanut.

62
Mr White

'ir?' said Alan, looking nervously at the screen. 'Is everything OK?'

'You call *that* an interrogation?' said the person on screen in an angry, surprisingly high voice.

'I-I-I've only just started.'

'Useless! If you want a job done properly, you've got to do it yourself!'

'You're Mr White,' said Peanut.

'Indeed,' said the silhouette, turning slightly to face her. 'And you are Pernilla Anne Jones.'

'Peanut!' she said, automatically. 'How do you know my name? And what have you done with my friends?'

'Your friends? Oh yes, the tall boy with the hair, the

annoying little girl and the scruffy mutt. They are currently enjoying my hospitality, just like you.' He laughed. 'Would you like to see them?'

Peanut nodded.

The screen cut to a shot of Rockwell in a cell just like the one Peanut was in. He was sitting on a chair with his head in his hands, rocking slowly back and forth. Five seconds later, it cut to another cell, but this time Peanut could see Doodle standing on his hind legs, his paws on the door, barking loudly. The final shot really upset Peanut. Her little sister was curled up on the cold concrete bench in her cell, quietly singing to herself. She could just about make out the words *'Twinkle, twinkle, little star . . . How I wonder what you are . . .'* A tear ran down Peanut's cheek.

'And Mr Markmaker?'

'He has been moved to an even more comfortable location.' The screen cut to a shot of Mr M in a cell that was half the size of the others. He was sitting perfectly still on the chair, staring straight at the huge type printed on the wall. *Poor man*, thought Peanut. *Maybe this was the final straw for him.*

'What are you going to do with us, you *monster*?' Peanut wiped the tears from her eyes but could not hide the anger in her voice.

'That depends on whether you cooperate,' sneered Mr White.

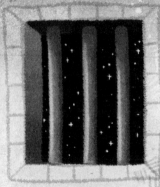

'What do you want?'

'I want to know how you got from London to Chroma. It must have either been through a portal, in which case I want to know exactly where that portal is, or . . . you used another method.'

Peanut shook her head. 'Why do you care so much?'

'Well, young lady, we can't have just anybody waltzing in here with their illegal drawing apparatus, directly disobeying my laws, can we? Where would that leave us?'

'In a much happier place!' shouted Peanut. 'Maybe it would leave us all with a much happier world!'

'Why on earth do you think the world would be happier with more creativity in it? The sooner people realise that a planet devoid of art means a more ordered, controlled and calm existence, the better.'

'Existence!' said Peanut. 'You do know that there is a difference

between merely existing and actually *living*, don't you?'

'OK, you're boring me now, young lady. I'm going to ask again. How. Did. You. Get. Here? Did you have help?' He pulled the brim of his hat down even further over his eyes. 'From your father, for example.'

Peanut felt the blood drain from her face. 'My father? What have you done to him? Where is he?'

'Oh bravo, Miss Jones. An Oscar-worthy performance. But enough with the pretending. Why don't you just tell me where he is right now, to avoid my having to use a more . . . painful method of extraction.'

'Er, what do you mean?' Peanut was confused. 'You know full well where he is. He's here. In the Spire. In a cell somewhere.'

'Don't toy with me, young lady!' snapped Mr White. 'Yes, he *was* imprisoned here, but he's not any more, as I think you know. He . . . disappeared a few days ago.'

'Disappeared?' Peanut felt as if her legs were going to buckle. 'What do you mean, "disappeared"?'

Mr White seemed thrown by this reaction. 'So, you *really* don't know where he is?'

Peanut shook her head.

Mr White then started laughing a terrible, high-pitched laugh. He sounded like a hyena who had sucked all the helium out of a balloon.

'Oh dear, oh dear.' Mr White dabbed at his eyes with a handkerchief. 'Here was I, hoping that you would be able to tell me how he escaped, but it seems we're both in the dark as far as your father's whereabouts are concerned.'

Suddenly, Peanut's surprise and confusion turned to anger. She realised that she was right back where she'd started – not knowing where her dad was. And it was all because of this man, who had put him in prison in the first place. She took a deep breath and began to gather her thoughts.

'So, if your father didn't help you,' sneered Mr White, 'how did you get here?'

Peanut glared at him and didn't say a word.

'I see. It's the silent treatment, is it? OK. Have it your own way.' Mr White picked up a folder from the desk in front of him and held it up to the camera. 'It would be much easier if you just told us. It would save us a lot of paperwork. And paper doesn't grow on trees, you know!'

Peanut's eyes widened. Something niggled in her memory, just out of reach.

'Alan!' barked Mr White. 'Make sure she's thoroughly searched before you leave her to think about what she's done. I don't trust this girl.'

Searched? Peanut looked around the room. She took a deep breath. Could she escape if

she was quick? She had to
take the risk. It was now
or never.

In a flash, she ripped
the makeshift pocket from
her dungarees and grabbed
Little Tail.

As soon as he
saw it, Mr White
gasped. 'Is that . . . ? No!
It can't be!'

As quickly as she could, Peanut drew a rectangle on the
wall next to her, but before she could sketch a door handle,
Alan was upon her. He grabbed her wrist, pulling the pencil
towards him. Peanut did her best to wrestle it back.

'CAREFUL!' bellowed Mr White from the TV screen.

But it was too late.

Alan suddenly let go of Peanut's arm, and the pencil flew
out of her hand. They both watched as it soared through
the air in slow motion towards the window and, to Peanut's
horror, sailed between the bars and out into the night sky.

'NOOOOOOOOOO!' screamed Peanut.

'NOOOOOOOOOO!' screamed Mr White.

Alan looked up at the TV screen in panic, sweat on his
brow. Peanut was breathing hard.

Mr White had grabbed a microphone, and was bellowing into it: 'PAGING all RAZER units. A small, yellow pencil has just fallen from floor ninety-nine of the Spire. It is an item of EXTREME importance. I repeat, EXTREME importance. Treat with care! IF IT BREAKS, ITS POWER IS DESTROYED. I am overriding all of your existing protocols. Your number one directive, your only directive, is to find THE PENCIL at all costs. THIS IS A CODE PURPLE! A CODE PURPLE!'

The TV screen suddenly went blank. Alan, clearly panicking, scrambled to his feet and ran out of the cell, slamming the door behind him.

Peanut heard Alan's footsteps fade into the distance and shook her head in disbelief. What was she going to do? The reality of her predicament began to sink in. Her dad was still missing and the yellow pencil, their only hope of escaping from the Spire and getting back home, had gone forever.

63
Old Friends

Peanut lay on the concrete bench staring at the ceiling. She couldn't remember another time when she had felt this hopeless. Even the weeks immediately after her dad had left weren't this bad. Despite the fact that she had lived for twelve and a quarter years unaware that the yellow pencil even existed, she was now finding it hard to imagine life without it. Not least because it had always, throughout this entire adventure, been their ticket back home.

Home.

80 Melody Road had been a pretty unhappy place for the past year. Dad wasn't there, Mum always seemed angry about something, and her brother didn't talk to her any more. Her

only comfort had been her drawing and painting, and now Mum was doing her best to take that away from her.

Lying there, alone in a prison cell several hundred metres above the Illustrated City, she whispered, 'I need you, Dad. I need your help now more than ever.'

She sniffed, looked at the paint-splatter stars through the cell window, and listened to the rhythmic flutter of the leaves as the wind danced through the forest canopy. Her head was swimming. At that moment, she would have given anything for her mum to walk through the door, give her a cuddle and tell her that everything was going to be OK.

Wait a second!

She sat bolt upright, held her breath and listened again.

'We're ninety-nine floors up. That fluttering noise can't be leaves. No tree is that tall,' she said out loud.

She scrambled to her feet, jumped on to the bench, stood on tiptoe and put her face to the small window.

And what she saw made her heart leap.

There, hovering on the other side of the bars of Peanut's cell window,

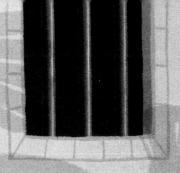

were three kaleidoscoppi.
One had a red crest on
his head, one green and
one gold. Their rainbow
wings, beating hard, were
a multicoloured blur as the great birds hung in the air.

'It's you!' said Peanut, smiling. 'I set you free back in the
North Draw!'

They nodded.

Then something very strange happened. The red-and-
green-topped birds looked straight into Peanut's eyes and
trilled several bars of a beautiful, mesmeric melody, causing a
warm, tingly feeling to spread from the top of her head to the
tips of her toes.

In an instant, all of her feelings of despair vanished and
were replaced by something new. Something she hadn't felt
in a while.

Hope.

She couldn't explain how or why, but she felt sure that
her dad was OK. Somehow, he'd managed to escape from
the Spire and make his way to a safer place. If only she knew
where. She smiled at the kaleidoscoppi.

'You helped him, didn't you? You helped him to escape,'
she said.

The birds didn't respond but their song continued to

swoop and soar. It filled Peanut's heart. Then she noticed that the gold-topped bird wasn't singing. He was holding something in his beak. Something eighteen centimetres long and bright yellow.

Peanut could hardly believe her eyes.

'Little Tail!' she gasped.

64
Escape

She reached through the bars and carefully took the pencil from gold-top's beak.

'How can I ever thank you?' she said.

The three birds sang several bars in perfect three-part harmony, nodded in unison and then disappeared into the night.

Peanut watched them go with a big smile on her face. Then she climbed down from the bench, walked across her cell and put her ear to the door. Nothing. This was her chance. She had to act fast.

Taking the pencil in her left hand, she first drew a keyhole in the door. Then, in the air in front of her, she drew a key. She plucked the key from mid-air, put it in the keyhole, turned it and, as quietly as she could, opened the door.

She poked her head out into the corridor. There was no sign of movement. The RAZER guards must have left their posts to go and look for the pencil. The pencil that she was now holding in her hand.

'Right. Focus, Peanut,' she said to herself. She thought hard about the film that Mr White had shown her of Rockwell, Little-Bit, Doodle and Mr M in their cells. That had been a huge mistake on his part. In fact, she couldn't quite believe he'd done it. The huge black type on the walls that denoted the cell number had been clearly visible in each shot, so it was now just a question of Peanut remembering them.

The good news was that they had all started with 'F99', meaning they were on the ninety-ninth floor. Rockwell's was the closest to her cell: C32, only five doors away. She tiptoed down the curving corridor until she was standing in front of Cell 32. Then, as before, she drew a lock and key and opened the door.

Rockwell was standing by the bench, legs slightly bent and arms raised as if ready to fight. When he saw it was Peanut, his face lit up and he ran to hug her.

'You did it!' he said.

'*Sssshhh*,' she whispered. 'We can't afford for anyone to hear us.'

Rockwell grabbed his rucksack and followed her out of the door.

Next was Doodle in Cell 21. His entire body wagged when he saw Peanut and Rockwell.

Little-Bit was further around the circular passageway in Cell 5. Peanut had remembered the number because it matched her younger sister's age.

'Peeeeeaaaaaannnnuuuuutttttttt,' she squeaked as they burst into her cell. 'I knew you'd rescue me.'

Now they just had to find Mr M.

'He's in C1,' said Peanut as they tiptoed along the corridor. 'Here it is.'

Just as she was putting her drawing of a key into her drawing of a lock, they heard the *ding* of the elevator a few doors to their right.

'Quick. Inside!' whispered Peanut, before opening the cell door, shoving the others through it, diving inside herself and closing it behind her.

65
Floor Ninety-Nine, Cell One

The tiny room was now crammed with people, all holding their breath. Little-Bit was sitting on the floor, Rockwell was wedged between the bed and the wall with the type on it, Peanut was standing with her back against the door, and sitting on the chair with a very waggy Doodle on his lap was Malcolm Markmaker.

'You again,' he said. 'Are you all OK? I saw what happened to you. How did you escape?'

'There's no time for that,' whispered Peanut urgently. 'We've got to get out of here before Mr White and the RAZERs realise we're not in our cells.'

'What about the other prisoners?' said Rockwell. 'And your dad?'

'Your *dad*?' said Mr M.

'Yes. Gary Jones. Apparently he isn't here any more. He escaped a couple of days ago. And we'll have to come back for the other prisoners,' said Peanut. 'Right now, the most important thing is getting Mr M here back to Mrs M. You remember what she said: he is essential to the Resistance and their fight against Mr White.'

'Mrs M?' cried Mr M. 'You've met my wife?'

'How do you think we knew you were here?' said Peanut, smiling.

Suddenly, they heard metallic voices coming from just outside the cell door.

'I think there are RAZERs outside. We're trapped,' said Little-Bit.

'We're going to need to take the quick way down,' said Peanut.

'Er, what's the quick way down?' asked Rockwell nervously.

66
The Quick Way Down

Peanut took the pencil out of her pocket and drew a can of spray paint as carefully as she could, trying to remember what the one in her (now confiscated) bandolier had looked like. When she finished, she picked it up.

Mr M gasped. 'Is that . . . is that . . . Pencil Number One?'

'It is,' said Peanut, before picking up her drawing and testing the spraying mechanism. She aimed the nozzle at the wall. It worked perfectly.

She smiled. 'OK. I think we've got a chance . . .' she said excitedly.

Then she drew a big, dotted-line oval that stretched from high up on the wall right down to the floor. When she had finished, she told everyone to stand back. She steeled herself for a moment, and then kicked the middle of the circle as hard as she could. To everyone's surprise, the whole thing popped out and tumbled into the night, as if the dotted lines she'd drawn were perforations. There was now a massive hole in the wall.

The purple, star-filled sky looked huge as the wind rushed noisily into the room. The sudden sound triggered a commotion outside their cell: metallic voices talking very fast. Then they heard the sound of a key in the lock.

'Quick!' shouted Peanut. 'Everyone stand in single file behind me and grab the person in front.' Mr M scooped up Doodle and they all did as they were told.

The cell door started to open.

'Hold tight!'

Peanut stood looking out of the hole into the void, her toes over the edge of the precipice and the wind blowing through her topknot. She held the can of spray paint in front of her, pointed it just ahead of her feet, and pushed the button. A wide blast of paint came flying out of the nozzle, creating a length of runway suspended in the air in front of them. Peanut smiled. Then she aimed the can slightly further ahead and started to shape the runway so that it began to slope downwards like a slide. She edged the whole group out of the hole and along the first section of spray paint. When they reached the beginning of the incline, she held her breath and tipped her body forwards.

WHOOSH!

They all started to zoom down the chute, standing upright like a conga line of Silver Surfers. As they whizzed along, Peanut kept her finger on the button, spraying a pathway a couple of metres ahead of them. It twisted and turned like a magical ribbon in the sky.

After thirty seconds or so, Peanut began to get the hang of it. In a moment of science-based rationale that even Death

Breath Dawkins would have been proud of, she decided that flying in circles would be the best way of modulating their speed and maintaining a certain amount of control. So she started to circle the Spire as if it were a giant helter-skelter.

'THIS IS LIKE THE BEST ROLLER COASTER EVER!' whooped Little-Bit.

Rockwell and Mr M, on the other hand, looked decidedly ill.

'Are we nearly there yet?' asked Rockwell gingerly.

'We're about a quarter of the way down,' replied Peanut, marvelling at the magnificent view.

It was something to behold. Even though it was night-time, she could see the clearly defined districts radiating out from the Spire, rotating below them as they circled the tower: the long, straight bridge of Die Brücke, the patchwork farmland of Vincent Fields, the ponds of the Light District, the skyscrapers of Superhero Heights, the highways of the Strip and the black mountains of the Ink District.

When the North Draw came into view, she aimed the spray paint slightly to the right and straightened their descent, aiming for the wide-open snowy expanses. As they flew over the north side of the Rainbow Lake, Peanut felt a sudden wave of relief. She shouted over her shoulder, 'I think we're going to make it. I think we're going to be OK!'

Unfortunately, she had spoken too soon.

67
The Snowfields of the North Draw

As the party of five slid to the ground, finally reaching the snowfields of the North Draw, it appeared that their daring escape from the Spire had gone totally unnoticed.

'Mr White and the RAZERs must *really* want to find my pencil,' said Peanut.

'What do you mean?' asked Rockwell as Peanut busily drew a lantern to shed some light on the proceedings. 'How do they know about the pencil?'

She spent the next five minutes explaining everything that had happened during her encounter with Mr White and

Alan up on the ninety-ninth floor.

'Wow!' said Rockwell. 'The kaleidoscoppi turned up to help? It just goes to show that if you give a little love, it really does all come back to you.'

'Indeed,' said Mr M. 'You reap what you sow, as Mr White will discover sooner rather than later, hopefully.'

The three children turned to face the man that they had been charged with rescuing.

'It's lovely to meet you, finally,' said Peanut. Doodle licked Mr M's face.

'Likewise. And I can't thank you enough for rescuing me.' He smiled. 'Let's head back to HQ, where we can at least sort you out with a cup of tea. That would be a start. Now, I'd say that it would be wise to get out of sight as soon poss—'

Before he could finish the sentence, a familiar high-pitched sound filled the night sky. The group turned to look back towards the Spire and saw what looked like a huge, glittering silver cloud on the horizon. But, as it rolled towards them, twinkling in the moonlight, it soon became apparent that it wasn't a cloud at all, rather a huge shoal of Exocetia, the mechanical flying fish. They were travelling low across the ground, directly towards the group, and they were moving fast. Very fast.

'Er, I think it's time to go,' said Rockwell.

'I concur,' said Mr M.

'RUN!' shouted Little-Bit.

But, seconds later, the cloud was upon them.

The first few Exocetia flew straight past them like bullets, before stopping fifty metres ahead, turning around and forming a long, curved barrier. Seconds later, Peanut, Rockwell, Little-Bit, Mr M and Doodle found themselves in the middle of the vast shoal.

The group stopped running and stood in a tight circle facing out, with their hands over their ears, as thousands of screaming fish, their eyes glowing red, joined the throng.

Then, all of a sudden, the wailing stopped.

Silence.

Peanut felt a light fluttering sensation in the pit of her stomach. Then the vibration moved to her chest as a barely audible hum began to increase in volume. The snow on the ground oscillated as the hum got louder and louder and louder, eventually rising to a thundering roar. Then the wall of fish surrounding them parted to reveal the enormous, monstrous, terrifying vehicle responsible for the noise.

The children had never seen anything like it in their lives. It was huge: as tall as a house and as wide as a tennis court. It was supported by two enormous sets of tank tracks that rolled slowly but relentlessly, dragging their huge cargo across the snow. The central part was made up of several rivet-covered boxes, on top of which sat a large cockpit with a narrow, black

windscreen. Just behind that were several floodlights that lit the whole area, and a huge vat, emblazoned with a large white 'X', with five little chimneys sticking out of the top. Each one was billowing a plume of jet-black smoke. But the pièce de résistance, the truly terrifying icing on the already-pretty-

scary cake, was the front of the vehicle. It literally had a mouth – a huge opening, ten metres wide, lined, top and bottom, with pointed, razor-sharp metal teeth that moved up and down very, very quickly. And if that wasn't enough, inside the mouth was a rapidly rotating cylinder covered with hundreds more tooth-like blades.

'The Big X,' whispered Rockwell.

'Oh dear!' gasped Little-Bit.

'Er, Peanut,' said Rockwell. 'There's a massive, horrifying, metal eating-machine approaching us. Any ideas?'

She studied the Big X as it rolled towards them. When it was about ten metres away from the group, it slowed to a standstill and the engine stopped. A gullwing door opened to the right of the windscreen, and a large block of metal emerged hydraulically. It gradually unfolded to reveal itself as a flight of stairs. When the bottom tread reached the ground, a figure dressed all in dazzling white and topped with a fedora stepped from the cockpit and walked down the steps. He was followed by the muscular figure of Alan. They approached Peanut.

'Miss Jones,' said the man in the hat.

'Mr White,' said Peanut.

68
Face to Face

He was much shorter than she'd imagined. However, Peanut couldn't deny that, in the flesh, Mr White had quite a presence. He appeared to be made of actual light, which made him seem otherworldly. He positively shone, so much so that Rockwell and Little-Bit had to shield their eyes. Peanut couldn't see his face because of the glare, but she could just about make out the shape of the fedora hat that she'd seen on the video screen in her cell.

'Well, Miss Jones,' he said in his high tenor, 'up until an hour ago, you were just another annoying member of the Resistance that had to be . . . dealt with.' He looked back over his shoulder at the blades of the Big X. 'But certain . . . details have recently come to light that have . . . changed things somewhat.'

'And what might those be, *White*?' Mr M stepped out from behind Rockwell and stood next to Peanut. Several flying fish inched forward. Mr White held up his hand to halt them.

'Ah, Markmaker, aka the brains behind the entire Resistance movement, aka our most valuable prisoner. And yet here you are, free. Alan has, yet again, excelled himself with his peerless attention to security, I see.'

Alan's face flushed.

'And not only that,' Mr White continued. 'Earlier this evening, I saw something that I never thought I would see. Something I thought was either a myth or had been lost long ago.'

'Your morals?'

'Witty,' deadpanned Mr White. 'A veritable comedian. You, young lady, were in possession of Conté's Pencil. Pencil Number One. Little Tail. Do you deny it?'

Peanut didn't react.

'You have no idea how powerful that pencil is, do you? It is wasted on you!' He was shouting now. 'If I had Conté's pencil, you would not believe what I could achieve!'

He took a deep breath to regain his composure.

'Anyway, that is all by the by, because, unfortunately, due to my assistant's continuing stupidity –' Alan's face was now scarlet – 'the item in question fell from the Spire.'

'That's right. It did. Well done, Alan,' Peanut said. Alan scowled back at her. 'So you've not found it then? I thought you had all of your robots searching the place.'

'I did. In fact, the RAZERs are still scouring the area as we speak. As yet they have not been successful in locating the pencil.'

'Oh well. As you said, you didn't think it even existed an hour ago. I'd just let it go if I were you.'

'The thing is,' said Mr White, 'when we returned to the Spire and discovered that you and your friends were no longer in your cells, we were, naturally, curious as to how you'd managed to escape. That's when we spotted your little chute. Quite ingenious.'

'Why, thank you,' said Peanut, trying not to show that she was feeling more nervous by the second.

'The puzzling thing, however, is that we still have your contraband art materials.' He gestured to Alan, who held up

Peanut's bandolier. 'So, what I am wondering is . . . how did you manage to spray-paint your way out of the tower, if you didn't have anything to spray-paint with?'

'That's easy. I had this.' Peanut threw the pencil-drawn spray can so that it landed at Mr White's feet. 'You missed it when you searched me.'

'Hmmm.' He bent down to pick it up. 'It's highly unlikely that the RAZERs would have missed something of this size.'

He broke off the nozzle of the can and rubbed it between his fingers. 'Curiouser and curiouser,' he muttered.

'What do you mean?' said Peanut.

'Well, strangely, this can is made of graphite. Pencil graphite. A very dense, very good quality pencil graphite. In fact, it's like no pencil graphite I have ever seen before.'

Peanut shifted her weight from foot to foot. Mr M and Rockwell inched closer to her.

'Do you know what I think?' Mr White smiled. 'I think that you, Miss Jones, drew this spray-paint can with Conté's Pencil.'

'Impossible!' Peanut laughed. 'You saw it fly out of the window. You just said so yourself.'

'Nevertheless, I think it would be prudent for us to search you. Exocetia! Surround her!'

At least a hundred of the spiky robots darted towards Peanut, but Mr M, Rockwell, Little-Bit and Doodle were quicker. They surrounded Peanut to stop the fish from getting too close.

'Ha ha ha! You think that will stop us?' Mr White laughed.

Peanut knew he was right. She took a deep breath. It was finally time to play the only hand left open to her.

'Call them off!' she shouted. 'Call them off NOW!'

Mr White smiled. He could see that Peanut was holding Little Tail high above her head. It gleamed in the moonlight. 'And why would I do that?'

Peanut looked straight at Mr White. 'Because, if you don't call them off, I will snap the pencil. Its power will be gone forever. And don't think I won't do it . . .'

Mr White was silent for a second. 'All right,' he said calmly. 'Exocetia, retreat.'

The fish moved back.

'So this is how it's going to work,' said Peanut. 'You are going to let me and my friends go. We are going to walk away and you are going to let us. If you don't, I will destroy this pencil.'

Mr White considered what she'd said.

'I don't believe you. I know what that pencil can do. I've read the books about Conté and I know that it can create portals and many, many other things.'

Peanut looked worried.

'So . . . in terms of how you and your little friends arrived in Chroma: mystery solved. That pencil is your ticket home.

Not even you would be so stupid as to destroy your own escape route.'

'And what, exactly, do I have to go home to? My dad has gone . . . my mum doesn't like me . . . I hate my school. Let's just say that I'm not feeling overly homesick! I have nothing more to lose. I made a promise to return Mr M to the Resistance and I intend to keep it, so let us go.'

Mr White took a step forward.

'I warned you!' said Peanut, holding the pencil as if she were about to snap it.

'ALL RIGHT! All right! Stop!' shouted Mr White. 'Just – just go.'

Peanut looked at Mr M. She looked at Rockwell and Little-Bit.

Then, very slowly, she started walking backwards, away from Mr White, still holding the pencil in front of her. The others started to walk backwards too. Mr White flicked a hand, and the shoal of fish behind them parted.

As they backed away, Peanut looked over at Mr M. He looked back at her.

'So . . .' he said. 'Now what?'

69
One Final Sketch

The group kept retreating until they were a good couple of hundred metres away. The Big X still looked huge, as did the cloud of robotic fish. Peanut could see Mr White, still glowing in the night air, whispering to Alan.

'Mr M, how long will it take us to get to the bunker from here?' asked Rockwell.

'Walking backwards at this pace, about a day and a half!'

'Oh.'

Peanut wracked her brains. 'OK, you four stand guard. I'm going to draw us something to speed things along a bit.'

Peanut crouched down, and started sketching.

'Er, Peanut. Something's happening . . .' said Little-Bit.

'What?'

'I'm not sure, but Mr White is talking to one of the fishes and pointing at us.'

'I'm nearly done . . .' A minute later, she stood up. 'What do you think?'

There in the snow, were two very basic outlines of scooters, similar to the one she'd drawn back on the Strip. This time, however, instead of wheels, they had huge jet rockets sticking out of the sides of the footplates.

'Something's definitely happening back there,' said Rockwell. 'PEANUT, LOOK OUT!'

70
The Chase, Part II

he Exocetia shot out of the shoal at such a speed that Peanut didn't even have a chance to react. The supersonic fish flew through the air like an arrow, almost knocking the pencil from Peanut's hand, before arcing around in a semi-circle and returning to Mr White. The whole thing took about three seconds.

The children blinked.

Doodle barked.

Mr M leaped into action. 'LET'S GO!'

He jumped on to one of the scooters with Doodle and Little-Bit. Rockwell and Peanut took the other one.

'There's a button on the jet!' shouted Peanut. She and Mr M bent down, pressed the small, round knobs, and the two vehicles shot forwards. Peanut was surprised at the acceleration.

'WHOOOOOOO-HOOOOOOO!' screamed Little-Bit.

Mr M steered his scooter in front of Peanut's and yelled 'FOLLOW ME!' over his shoulder. He immediately veered to the left towards a wooded area as yet untouched by the Big X.

Suddenly, they were surrounded by lots of flying fish that appeared next to them out of thin air, as if they were X-wing fighters exiting hyperspace. Peanut realised with terror that she was still holding Little Tail and gripped it as tightly as she could.

'INTO THE TREES!' yelled Mr M. They swooped down a slope and flew into the woods.

As the two jet-powered scooters weaved between the trunks, one fish after another flew at Peanut. They were tracking her. A few of them clattered into tree trunks with metallic thunks before exploding into balls of flame. Rockwell's eyes widened.

'OMG! I forgot about that!' he shouted.

'Forgot about what?' yelled Peanut.

'Er, don't worry. You just concentrate on avoiding the trees!'

He pulled his rucksack from his back and desperately rifled through the front pocket.

Meanwhile, Mr M was zigging and zagging with astonishing accuracy. Lots of short, sharp turns, dipping under branches, flying over roots, 180-degree spins, neck-whipping chicanes at breakneck speeds. Both he and Little-Bit looked like they were having the time of their lives.

Peanut was doing her best to keep up with him, but she wasn't enjoying it as much. Mainly because she was having to deal with the Exocetia, whose sole aim appeared to be staying as close to her and the pencil as possible.

'Keep holding them off!' shouted Rockwell. 'It must be here somewhere!'

'What must?'

'That device that Jonathan Higginbottom gave me! The one that blows up the fish!'

Suddenly, the two scooters were out of the woods and

back on the open plains. As they flew across the hills and valleys of the North Draw, Mr M shouted across to Peanut.

'WE'RE NEARLY THERE! WE NEED TO SHAKE THEM OFF BEFORE WE GET TO THE BUNKER, IF WE CAN!'

'OK!' she replied. 'Rockwell, we're running out of time! Hurry.'

As they crested a particularly large hill, Peanut suddenly noticed a touch of colour in the distance. It was hard to miss because everything else in the North Draw was so monochrome. And then she spotted some movement. It looked like . . . people. Yes. There were lots of people and they were building something. Something big. Something . . . pink and blue.

'WHAT'S GOING ON?' yelled Peanut.

'I'LL TELL YOU WHAT'S GOING ON,' replied Mr M. 'MY WIFE, THAT'S WHAT'S GOING ON!'

Peanut batted away yet another Exocetia as it got dangerously close.

'WHAT DO YOU MEAN?'

'I KNEW SHE WOULDN'T LET US DOWN!' beamed  Mr M. 'SHE'S MOBILISED THE RESISTANCE!'

71
The Resistance

As they flew down into the valley on their jet-propelled scooters, they had a fantastic view of the entire scene.

Forming a massive circle that stretched across the entire width of the North Draw were hundreds of large, spiky interlocked crosses embedded in the snow. They looked just like the Second World War anti-tank obstacles that Peanut had seen on a Melody High school trip to the beaches of Normandy, except that these were all either bright pink or bright blue. 'Czech hedgehogs', they were called. Peanut remembered the name because you would expect such a creature to be cute and friendly. These things, however, did not look cute and they certainly didn't look friendly. They could stop even the biggest tank, even one as huge as the Big X. The Resistance meant business!

But that wasn't all. Within the enormous circle of pink and blue Czech hedgehogs was a huge, dome-like structure. They didn't notice it at first, but as they got closer, Peanut could see that it was made entirely of a very close netting, drawn in blue coloured pencil. Standing just inside the netting were lots of people. And one huge alligator.

'JONATHAN HIGGINBOTTOM!' shouted Little-Bit.

Three more flying fish swooped at Peanut. As she jerked out of the way, the scooter veered off sharply to the left and almost flipped over.

'THAT WAS A CLOSE ONE!' she yelled.

'LOOK! TO THE RIGHT!' shouted Mr M. 'IT'S MILLICENT!'

Sure enough, Peanut could see Mrs M beckoning them towards a small opening in the netting. Mr M, Little-Bit and

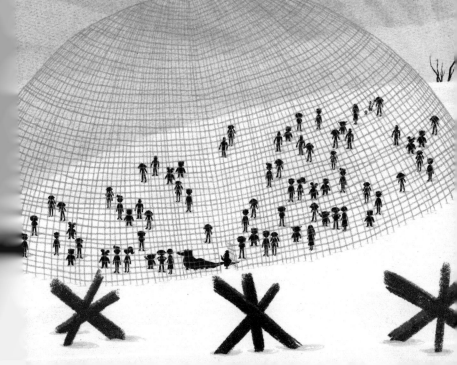

Doodle immediately headed towards it. Peanut followed, fifty metres behind, with about a hundred Exocetia on her tail. She watched the other scooter fly through the entrance.

'ROCKWELL!' she shouted. 'I THINK WE'RE GOING TO MAKE IT!'

72
BOOM!

There was nothing she could have done about it.

It was a perfect storm of unfortunate events.

First, Peanut's control of the speeding scooter was only partial, since she was having to swerve this way and that to avoid the Czech hedgehogs that dotted the ground between them and the safety of the netted dome.

Second, the appearance of the Big X at the top of the

valley had sent huge vibrations across the snow which had added considerable wobble to the proceedings.

And third, Rockwell had finally managed to press the button on Jonathan Higginbottom's anti-Exocetia device just as a hundred of the flying fish had closed in on Peanut's scooter. This was arguably the biggest contributor to what happened next.

The explosion was huge. The scooter and its riders were sent flying, high into the air, landing in the soft snow several metres apart with a thump. That many mechanical fish all blowing up at the same time is quite a thing, it turns out.

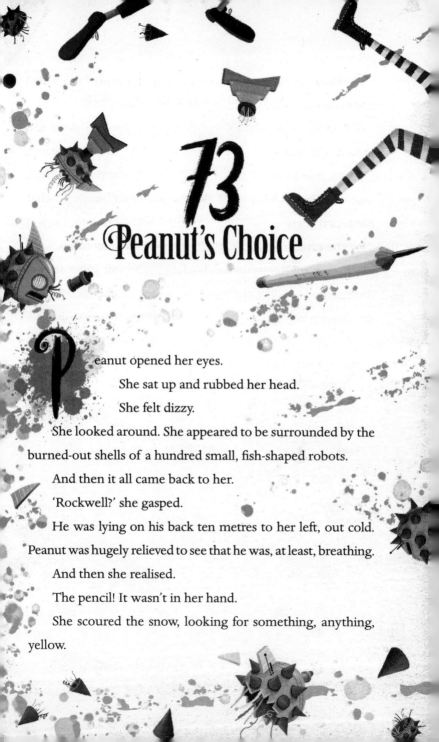

73

Peanut's Choice

eanut opened her eyes.

She sat up and rubbed her head.

She felt dizzy.

She looked around. She appeared to be surrounded by the burned-out shells of a hundred small, fish-shaped robots.

And then it all came back to her.

'Rockwell?' she gasped.

He was lying on his back ten metres to her left, out cold. Peanut was hugely relieved to see that he was, at least, breathing.

And then she realised.

The pencil! It wasn't in her hand.

She scoured the snow, looking for something, anything, yellow.

And there it was. Ten metres in the other direction. The most important pencil in the world, lying there in the snow.

Suddenly, she became aware that the ground all around her was shaking.

She looked up to see the Big X coming to a stop nearby.

She saw Mr White, radiating light, racing down the mechanical steps, closely followed by Alan. 'The boy has the anti-Exocetia weapon! Get him!' Mr White commanded.

Peanut looked at the pencil. Mr White was running towards it.

She looked at Rockwell. Alan was running towards him.

She only had time to save one of them.

She made her decision surprisingly quickly.

74
Sacrifice

Peanut heaved the unconscious Rockwell over her shoulder and hauled him as fast as she could towards Mr and Mrs M and the opening in the netting. She heard heavy footsteps behind her. It was Alan.

Suddenly, Doodle came racing out from inside the dome and ran straight for Mr White's henchman, barking as loudly as he could.

'Aaaargggh!' shrieked Alan, backing away. 'Nice doggy! Good doggy! Please don't hurt me!'

He turned around and ran back towards the Big X.

Peanut, still carrying Rockwell, stumbled through the opening into the dome, closely followed by Doodle.

'Well hello again, young lady,' said Jonathan Higginbottom. 'Allow me to help you with your friend. Let's get him some medical attention.'

Relieved, Peanut smiled as Mr and Mrs M helped her to lower Rockwell on to the alligator's back.

'Peanut!' beamed Mrs M. 'You did it, dear! You rescued Malcolm. Right! Let's get to the Bunker quickly, shall we? Cups of tea all round?'

As they rushed towards the little wooden hatch next to the tree-stump chimney, slap bang in the middle of the dome, Peanut looked back over her shoulder. She saw Mr White bending down to pick the pencil up. He stood up straight, cradling it in both hands. And then he started to laugh. Quietly at first, but then louder. Much louder.

'IT'S MINE!' he bellowed. 'CONTÉ'S PENCIL IS MINE!'

He turned around, seemingly oblivious to anything else, climbed the steps of the Big X, jumped into the cockpit and sat next to the trembling Alan. The terrible roar of the engine filled the valley before the vehicle turned around and drove away.

Peanut's eyes filled with tears. Yes, her friends were safe, for now, but her dad was still missing, and Little Tail was gone. And, with it, any chance they had of getting home.

Part Five

...in which Peanut really
wants to go home

75

Back in the Bunker

The heat from the roaring fire in the Bunker's circular living room felt more welcome than ever.

Peanut was sitting in an armchair sipping from a large mug of tea, with Little-Bit on her lap and Doodle at her feet. All around them, people were pulling books from shelves and packing them into the large, labelled cardboard boxes that were piled high around the room.

'So, where will the new headquarters be?' asked Peanut.

'Well, we have a few options,' replied Mrs M from the kitchen. 'The good news is that Mr White and the RAZERs seem to have gone – for the time being at least. It won't take us long to pack everything up and, as soon as we have, we will move to the new location.'

Mrs M smiled as she walked through the triangular doorway holding a tray of hot crumpets. 'By the way, Rockwell is going to be just fine.' She set the tray down next to Peanut. 'We were worried that he might have a concussion because he wouldn't stop talking nonsense: something about "triple maths" and "differentiation", but it turns out that he's just a bit worried about school. Totally normal for a boy of his age.'

'Did you tell him about the pencil? About the fact that we can't get back home?' asked Peanut.

'Now, why would I have told him something like that?'

'Because it's true. That pencil was our only way out of here.'

At that moment, Mr M strolled into the room and warmed his hands over the fire. Peanut leaned forward.

'Hello, Peanut,' he said. 'No word from your father, I'm afraid. We've put the word out with our best agents, but we've heard nothing yet.'

Peanut slumped back in her chair.

Mr M smiled kindly and walked over. 'Listen, my girl, your dad has proved his resourcefulness many, many times during his long service with the Resistance. For that reason, I firmly believe that he's OK. I'd wager that, as we speak, he's hiding from Mr White and the RAZERs somewhere in the city. If I know Gary, he'll be biding his time until an opportunity to move arises. We just have to be patient.'

'Yes,' said Peanut. 'I think you're right. I can't explain why, exactly, I just do . . . Something in the kaleidoscoppi's song told me he was safe. And at least we know he was in the Spire until just a few days ago. I *knew* he would never leave us on purpose!'

'One thing I can promise you,' said the old man, 'is that we *will* find him. This city owes you a great debt, and we will do whatever we can to reunite you with your dad. You and your friends are fully fledged members of the Resistance now, and we always look after our own.'

'Speaking of which,' said Mrs M, 'we have a proposition for you.'

'What is it?' Peanut was intrigued.

'Well, we wondered whether you would like to continue the work that your father was doing on our behalf.'

'The top-secret spying mission you told me about?' she said.

'The very same,' said Mrs M smiling. 'We suspect that there's some kind of link between your world and Mr White, and your dad was looking for evidence that might connect the two.'

Peanut flushed with pride. 'Well, if it was good enough for my dad, then that's good enough for me. I'm in.'

'But first, young lady, we need to get you back home to Melody Road,' said Mrs M. 'We don't want your mother to worry.'

Peanut looked confused.

'But . . . but . . . we can't go home! Mr White has Little Tail! How can I draw a door if I don't have Little Tail?'

'Ah yes. About that . . .' She rose from her chair and stood next to her husband. 'Peanut. Do you remember when you first arrived, I explained how the city of Chroma came into being all those centuries ago?'

'Yes.' Peanut nodded. 'You said it started with the Rainbow Lake.'

'That's right. And do you remember my mentioning people from the outside world, *your* world, coming to visit? Famous artists and creatives throughout history?'

'Yes.'

'Well, how do you think they got here?'

'I, er, I'm not sure. You said that there were rumours of portals between Chroma and the outside world, but you said they were never found.'

Mrs M turned to face Peanut. 'I'm embarrassed to say, I wasn't telling you the truth.'

'What do you mean?'

'Well, you see, we *know* that there is at least one portal,' said Mr M, smiling. 'It's a secret we guard closely, but we know exactly where it is.'

76
The Portal

They waited until daybreak.

Peanut stood in the Bunker's armoury waiting for Mr and Mrs M, Jonathan Higginbottom and Doodle, who were going to lead her, Rockwell and Little-Bit to the portal. She marvelled at the vast array of pink and blue pencils laid out in rows on the floor, all of which had been drawn by the original two that Mrs M still kept in her hair. Peanut took the sight of them as small consolation for the fact that she no longer had Little Tail to contribute to the cause.

Rockwell blustered into the room, his rucksack on his back and a bandage around his head. 'Are you ready, Peanut?'

'I am. How are you feeling?'

'Oh, I'm fine,' he replied. 'Hopefully the whack on the

head will have knocked a bit of sense into me. It's been quite the adventure, hasn't it?'

'Yes. It has. And you know what? There's no one else I'd rather have shared this experience with,' Peanut said, smiling. 'Now come on. Let's get going.'

The group left the bunker and headed north for the cover of Sketchwood, and then, once they were hidden by the trees, west.

Half an hour later they passed the signposts that Peanut had seen when she first arrived in Chroma. It seemed like a lifetime ago. After another hour of walking, the black, spiky trees of Sketchwood gradually became broader and leafier.

'The Green Valleys,' said Mr M. 'A beautiful, peaceful place. I only hope that it stays that way.'

Through gaps in the foliage, Peanut caught glimpses of rolling hills peppered with majestic oak trees stretching their branches up towards the sky.

'Here we are,' said Mrs M presently.

They were standing in the middle of a particularly densely wooded area, right on the city limits. Next to them was a narrow pathway that led into the thick greenery through a tunnel of trees.

'This is it. The Green Valleys portal.' Mr M pointed at the tunnel. 'Many famous creatives from your world have trodden this path. Hockney, Spencer, Sargent, your dad, to name but a few. You are in good company.'

'So . . .' said Peanut, 'I guess this is it. For now, at least.'

'It is. But we will be seeing you again,' said Mrs M. 'Of that, there is no doubt. And remember,

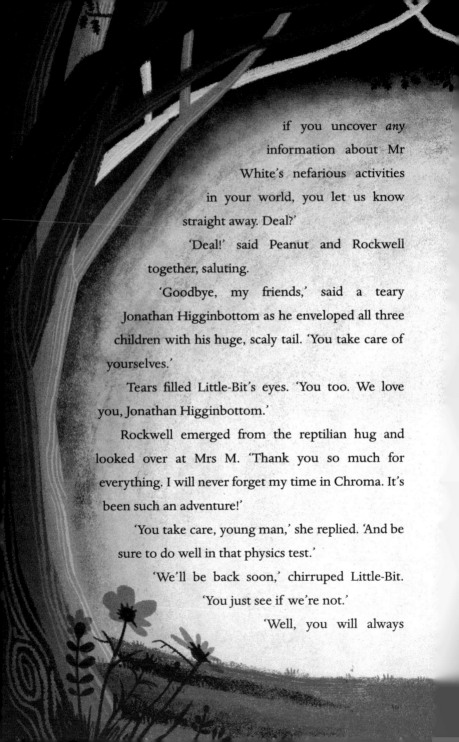

if you uncover *any* information about Mr White's nefarious activities in your world, you let us know straight away. Deal?'

'Deal!' said Peanut and Rockwell together, saluting.

'Goodbye, my friends,' said a teary Jonathan Higginbottom as he enveloped all three children with his huge, scaly tail. 'You take care of yourselves.'

Tears filled Little-Bit's eyes. 'You too. We love you, Jonathan Higginbottom.'

Rockwell emerged from the reptilian hug and looked over at Mrs M. 'Thank you so much for everything. I will never forget my time in Chroma. It's been such an adventure!'

'You take care, young man,' she replied. 'And be sure to do well in that physics test.'

'We'll be back soon,' chirruped Little-Bit. 'You just see if we're not.'

'Well, you will always

be welcome at the Bunker, wherever it may be. You have done the city of Chroma a great service by bringing Malcolm back to us.'

After more hugs and tears as they ruffled Doodle's soft, silky fur one last time, the children waved goodbye and started to make their way down the leafy passageway. The branches arching over their heads got lower the further they walked, so much so that they were almost bent double by the time they reached the door.

It was small and wooden – only about one metre high. Rockwell gave it a push. To their relief, it opened easily.

'You first,' he said to Peanut, wriggling aside to let her pass. 'See you on the other side . . .'

Peanut got down on her hands and knees, looked back over her shoulder at her sister and her best friend, and crawled through.

77

The National Portrait Gallery

he parquet floor on the other side of the door was cold. Peanut found herself wedged in a small gap between the opening and some kind of wooden plinth directly in front of her. She stood up. As she did so she bumped the plinth slightly, causing whatever it was holding to wobble worryingly. Instinctively, Peanut reached up to steady it. It was a marble bust.

Carefully, she edged out to find herself in a dimly lit room with very high ceilings and walls lined with large paintings.

'Where are we, Peanut?'

She turned to see Little-Bit emerge from behind the

bust, which she could now see was a sculpture of Queen Victoria.

'I'm not sure. An art gallery of some sort, I think.'

'Whoa, that was a bit of a squeeze,' said Rockwell as he slid his way out to join them in the rather ornate room. 'So, what is this place?'

'It's called an art gallery. I don't suppose you've ever visited one before, have you?'

'As it happens, I haven't. First time for everything though. It's, er, nice, isn't it?'

Peanut looked at her watch. 'No way,' she gasped.

'What?' said Rockwell.

'Well, according to my watch we've only been gone for about three hours!'

The children tiptoed their way through the deserted gallery. Just as they were passing a large portrait of the Duke and Duchess of Cambridge, a very tall security guard with huge shoulders and a neat white beard appeared at the end of the corridor. They froze. He appeared to be looking straight at them. The children held their breath . . .

A voice came from a room somewhere to the guard's left. 'Stanley! Do you want a cup of tea?'

To the gang's amazement, he turned towards it and shouted, 'Er, yes please. Milk and four sugars.' The guard looked back towards the children and Peanut could have sworn she saw the slightest hint of a smile play across his lips. Then he walked away.

'Phew! That was close,' said a relieved Rockwell.

The group carried on walking, careful not to make a sound, and eventually discovered a door that led them outside into the cool morning air. They found themselves on a busy street.

'We're in London!' shouted Little-Bit. 'Look!'

Sure enough, a couple of black cabs and a bright red bus drove past them towards a huge square to their right. It had a towering column in the middle of it, surrounded by statues of lions and topped with a solitary figure looking down over them.

'That's Nelson's Column,' said Peanut. 'We're right next to Trafalgar Square.' She looked behind her at the door they'd just come out of. 'Ah, so it's the National Portrait Gallery! That means Leicester Square tube station is just around the corner.'

She grabbed Little-Bit's hand.

'Come on, we're late for school.'

78
Home

For once, the tube journey was quick. They popped to Melody Road so that Peanut could change into her uniform. She ran up to her bedroom while Little-Bit and Rockwell waited downstairs.

Peanut looked around her room. She saw the drawing of the broken vase and the dead flower on her bed, the slightly damp Fantastic Four postcard on the wall, the empty piece of paper stuck to the wardrobe door, and the small pile of grey powder on the carpet beneath it.

Then she saw the wooden box full of Post-it notes. She couldn't quite believe that Little Tail wasn't in the secret compartment any more.

She thought about everything that she had seen in

Chroma and all the characters she had met: the kaleidoscoppi, the ink storm, Jonathan Higginbottom, the Bunker, Lulu Kawaii, the Rainbow Lake, the Markmakers, Table Guy, 72. How she wished she could tell her dad about it. He was the one person she wanted to share it all with.

'Soon,' she said under her breath. 'I'll tell you everything soon.'

As she folded up her dungarees, a piece of paper fell out of the pocket. It was the map of Chroma that Mrs M had given her. She picked it up and added a little drawing of a door and the words 'Queen Victoria, National Portrait Gallery' at the edge of the Green Valleys district. She wondered if there were any more portals elsewhere in the city. Maybe one day she would find out.

She put on her school uniform, headed back downstairs,

grabbed three apples from the fruit bowl and handed them out.

'Come on then,' she said to Rockwell and Little-Bit. 'Those lessons aren't going to learn themselves.'

The two friends dropped Little-Bit at her school before taking the shortcut to St Hubert's through the churchyard.

'Oh no! The physics test!' shouted Rockwell, startling Peanut so much that she almost dropped her apple.

'Er, *and* . . . ?'

'And . . . I HAVEN'T DONE AN ADEQUATE AMOUNT OF REVISION!'

'Well, I guess that's cos you've been too busy RESCUING PEOPLE AND HAVING AN AMAZING ADVENTURE!'

Rockwell ignored her.

'I *bet* Newton's Second Law comes up! Must remember . . . acceleration is *inversely* proportional to mass . . . acceleration is *inversely* proportional to mass . . . acceleration is *inversely* proportional to mass . . .'

Peanut couldn't help but laugh.

'What's so funny about not wanting a detention with Death Breath?'

'Nothing.' Peanut smiled. 'Nothing at all. Go on then, give me that textbook and I'll test you. But I'm warning you, if you get any questions wrong, I'm going to make you walk five metres behind me. Peanut Jones cannot be seen to be friends with a doofus.'

79
The Penny Drops

The day at school passed without incident. The teachers bought Peanut and Rockwell's explanations for being late – doctor (Peanut) and dentist (Rockwell) – and even the physics test went surprisingly well. Thermodynamics featured heavily and Peanut had to admit begrudgingly to Rockwell that she'd learned a thing or two from him during their time sketching hang-gliders back in the Ink District. She didn't tell him that she'd actually quite enjoyed doing the test. Neither Rockwell nor Peanut were ready for such an out-there revelation.

She got home just after four o'clock, grabbed herself a snack and plonked herself down on the sofa. Leo came in a few minutes later with Little-Bit.

'PEEEEEEAAAAAANNNNNNUUUUUTTTTTTTT!'

She ran into the living room and jumped on her big sister.

'I've not spoken about YOU-KNOW-WHERE to anyone at school today I've been soooo good I didn't even tell Marley.' She paused to catch her breath. 'Anyway, when are we going back?'

'Going back where?' asked Leo, suddenly interested.

'Oh, er, nowhere,' replied Peanut. 'It's just a game LB has invented.'

Leo looked at Peanut. His eyes narrowed slightly.

She shifted her position on the sofa.

'A game?' He shook his head. 'Right. Well, I'm going to my room.'

Five minutes later, the girls heard the sound of the key in the front door.

'I'M HOME!' shouted Mum from the hallway.

Hearing Mum's voice suddenly made Peanut realise how much she'd missed her. 'You're early!' she shouted, as she happily jumped up and ran into the hallway. She stopped dead in her tracks, however, when she saw who was standing next to her mother. It was somebody she'd forgotten all about.

'Hello there, Pernilla,' sneered Mr Stone in his high tenor. His piercing, pale grey eyes glinted as he looked her up and down as if seeing her for the first time. Peanut shuddered.

'Your mother, utterly charming woman that she is, has invited me to dinner.' He smiled, revealing a set of perfectly straight white teeth. 'I hope you don't mind. I wonder, would you be so kind as to take my hat and coat?'

Before she could answer, he flung his black jacket (with very, very, very dark grey stripes) at her, covering her head and shoulders entirely. She pulled it from her face to find that he was already holding out his hat for her to take. Peanut gasped. Somewhere deep inside her brain, a penny, that had been teetering on a precipice for quite some time, finally dropped.

Mr Stone's hat was a white fedora.

Epilogue

Two weeks later, Peanut was sitting with Rockwell in the dining hall. She didn't want to admit it, but she was enjoying having somebody to chat with every lunchtime, especially when that someone had also shared the adventure of a lifetime in Chroma.

'So,' said Rockwell, with a mouth full of tuna-and-jam sandwich, 'how did you get on?'

'I think it's finally ready,' replied Peanut. 'I've made quite a few improvements to the design. For starters, it's not made of dressing-gown cord. It's far more robust and waterproof. Now I just need to reload it with supplies.'

'Great!' Rockwell put a tick next to the word 'bandolier' in his notebook. 'So what are we waiting for?'

'Nothing. We're good to go to the National Portrait Gallery this weekend. I'll just tell Mum we're going to the Science Museum or something.'

'Cool. And Little-Bit?'

'I had to promise she could come, I'm afraid.'

'That's OK. It wouldn't be the same without her.'

Peanut opened her lunchbox and picked up a ham roll. She was just about to take a bite when she noticed something sticking out from underneath her fruit bar. Something yellow.

It was a Post-it note.

'I don't remember putting that there,' she whispered.

She pulled it out. Someone had drawn a thick, black 'L' shape on it.

Then she noticed something else. Tiny handwriting, just visible, running vertically along the edge of the note. She held the Post-it note a few centimetres from her face and squinted to read it.

And that's when everything changed.

Love you forever X

To be continued . . .

Follow Peanut as her search for Dad continues in

COMING IN AUTUMN 2022

About the Author

Rob Biddulph is a bestselling and multi award-winning author/illustrator whose books include *Blown Away*, *Odd Dog Out*, *Kevin* and *Show and Tell*. In March 2020 he started *#DrawWithRob*, a series of draw-along videos designed to help parents whose children were forced to stay home from school due to the coronavirus pandemic. The initiative garnered widespread international media coverage and millions of views across the globe. On 21 May 2020 he broke the Guinness World Record for the largest online art class when 45,611 households tuned in to his live *#DrawWithRob* YouTube class, and in July 2020 he was named as a Point of Light by the Prime Minister. He lives in London with his wife, their three daughters, Ringo the dog and Catface the cat. He is, for his sins, an Arsenal fan.

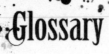

Glossary

Nicolas-Jacques Conté (1755–1805)

Nicolas-Jacques Conté was born in Normandy, France, and is the inventor of the modern pencil. He was also very interested in how the mechanics of flying worked. He even made his own hot-air balloon which he flew in the public square of his home town. Above all, he was an artist and produced portraits from which he made a lot of his money.

Die Brücke (founded in 1905)

Die Brücke, which translates in English to The Bridge, was the name given to a group of artists who worked in the German Expressionist Movement. This collective had a major impact on the evolution of modern art in Germany, and was mostly interested in people who felt lonely or different from those around them.

David Hockney (1937–present day)

David Hockney was born in Bradford but now divides his time between the USA and England. He is considered one of the most influential British artists of the twentieth century. His California paintings display a pop-art style and bright colours, a great example of which is the summery masterpiece *A Bigger Splash*. When back home in Yorkshire he likes to document, in paint or via digital art, the effect the seasons have on the landscape in works such as *Going Up Garrowby Hill*.

Gustav Klimt (1862–1918)

Gustav Klimt was an Austrian painter most famous for *The Kiss*. He used flat, decorative patterns of colour, and liked to focus on the human figure. Klimt himself was a great lover of cats. One of his many pets was named, imaginatively, Katze.

Oscar-Claude Monet (1840–1926)

Born in France, Monet was interested in nature and the French countryside. He liked to paint the same scenes over and over again, observing how its appearance changed throughout the day due to the changing light, and trying his best to capture

nature at its most realistic. He is probably most famous for 'Water Lilies', a series of approximately 250 paintings depicting his garden in Giverny, France.

National Portrait Gallery

The National Portrait Gallery opened in 1856 and has been located at its current site on St Martin's Place, near Trafalgar Square, London, since 1896. It is home to paintings, photographs and sculptures of some of the most historically important and famous British people, including William Shakespeare, the Brontë sisters and Queen Victoria.

Jackson Pollock (1912–1956)

Jackson Pollock was an American painter famous for his method of pouring and splashing paint all over the canvas. His most famous works include *Number 1 (Lavender Mist)*, and *Summertime: Number 9A*. He wasn't the most well-behaved student. In fact, he got expelled from school twice! Fun fact: his first name is actually Paul.

John Singer Sargent (1856–1925)

Born in Florence to American parents, John Singer Sargent developed his painting abilities in Paris before moving to London. He liked to paint watercolours of landscapes but is most famous for his elegant portraits in oil of Edwardian society. He was a master draftsman, and his ability to draw lyrically with a brush was incredible. He achieved worldwide fame and was fluent in four languages.

Sir Stanley Spencer (1891–1959)

Born in England, Stanley Spencer was best known for his paintings inspired by the Bible. He liked to present biblical scenes as if they were happening in his small home town of Cookham, beside the River Thames. In his later years, he produced many self-portraits and studies of his wife. His sensitivity to colour within the human form is almost unrivalled.

Vincent Van Gogh (1853–1890)

Vincent Van Gogh was born in the Netherlands and is one

of history's most influential artists. He worked in a post-impressionistic style, using bold colours and short, expressive brush-strokes. His best-known paintings include *Van Gogh's Chair* and *The Starry Night*. He is also famous for cutting his own ear off!

Andy Warhol (1928–1987)

Keen-eyed readers might have noticed that one of the Illustrated City's districts is called Warholia, named after the American artist Andy Warhol. Born in Pittsburgh, USA, he is famous for producing pop-art paintings and prints of, among other things, tins of Campbell's Condensed Tomato Soup, Mickey Mouse, bananas and Marilyn Monroe.

Acknowledgements

Publishing is a team sport. I'm just the glory-hunter who hangs around near the goal and gets to tap the ball into an empty net. So, with that in mind . . .

I'd like, firstly, to thank my agent, Jodie Hodges, to whom this book is dedicated. Not only did she do a brilliant job of drumming up an astonishing amount of interest in this, my first novel, but she is almost entirely responsible for getting my writing career off the ground back in 2014. So, y'know, cheers for that. Thanks too, to Emily Talbot and Molly Jamieson at United Agents for your support and hard work, especially during those crazy few weeks in the summer of 2019. You guys are the best and I feel very lucky to have you in my corner.

Fist-bumps and high-fives to Belinda Rasmussen and the entire team at Macmillan Children's Books. I really appreciate your faith in this story and your belief in me. You have made me feel very welcome and I'm so excited to be working with you all.

To Sarah Hughes, my editor, whose wise words, gentle prodding, eagle-eyed plot-hole-spotting and saint-like patience have made this whole process very enjoyable. They were right. You ARE amazing!

To design legends Chris Inns and Becky Chilcott. It can't be easy working with an ex-art director who always thinks he knows best, but you've made it seem so. Thanks for your amazing direction, for always being so positive, and for giving me the confidence and agency to express myself on the page. And thanks also to Tony Fleetwood for wrestling my unwieldy files into shape and making everything look beautiful.

Big thanks to Jeff Connell for his invaluable advice re corporate accountancy lingo. I knew being friends with a mathematical genius would pay off eventually.

To Maria Coole, my Welsh correspondent. *Diolch yn fawr iawn!*

To Mum and Dad. At a time when many parents weren't very keen on their children pursuing a career in the arts, you always got right behind me and my choices. Thank you so much for your unconditional support then, and your unconditional support now.

To the guinea-pig gang: Daniel and Martha Biddulph, and Alan and Lula Stainton. Thanks for reading that early draft and pretending that you liked it. It gave my fragile confidence a real boost. Bonus points to Alan for lending me his name. And his face.

To Leighann Pochetty for, all those years ago, coming up with the idea of putting a little Post-it note drawing into my youngest daughter's packed-lunch box when she was first starting school. That was the spark for this whole story.

To the booksellers, librarians, teachers, bloggers and reviewers who have supported me throughout my career. Thank you so much! I will never take your kind words for granted.

Thank you to my daughters Kitty and Poppy for their help on our National Portrait Gallery reconnaissance mission, and to Ella for the calmness. Peaceful fields, always.

And finally, thank you to my wife Ally. My first editor, my first reader, my sounding board and my co-conspirator. Thank you for always being there at my side, rain or shine, and for giving me the confidence and the freedom to do this. I love you. Oh, and thanks for giving Peanut her name.